I0846634

Snow Dust

Snow Dust

Book 1

Josh Decker

Names: Decker, Josh
Title: Snow Dust/Josh Decker

Summary: Snow is a young girl who must walk through a world filled with uncertainty. As echoes of her past slowly make their way to her.

Identifiers: ISBN # 979-8-9895137-3-4 (Paperback)
Subjects: / CYAC: / Magic – Fiction – Romance

ISBN # 979-8-9895137-4-1(Hardcover) — ISBN # 979-8-9895137-5-8 (Ebook)

First Edition

Printed in the United States of America

For my community that helped make this story possible. This story became more than I could ever imagine thanks to all of you.

Snow Dust

Chapter 1

"Ugh, why can't I get it to skip more than three times?" she growled, as she skipped another stone into the large pond before her.

Today had been yet another tough day for her. She was scolded by her teachers again, and she couldn't even eat lunch properly because everyone was bothering her.

Every day felt like another terrible ordeal in her life. Every time things begin to look up for her, they would end up like this.

Everywhere she went, she felt like nothing would change, which filled her with dread. She kept trying to improve her life, but the more she fought, the deeper her depression grew.

The only place where these feelings didn't show up was at this pond. It was nothing special—just a simple pond in the middle of the woods. But whenever she came here, her worries washed away.

Today was just another day she needed to vent her frustrations. But it seemed like she wasn't alone today.

Huh? Hey there, little guy," she said, noticing a cute white bunny at her feet. "This is my first time seeing you around here. Did you come out here to relax as well?"

The bunny looked at her innocently before nibbling on what seemed to be a carrot below its mouth. Sitting next to it, she couldn't help but find herself staring at it, wondering what it would be like to be a carefree animal like this.

If she were a bunny, she wouldn't need to worry about anything except enjoying her life.

Wanting to get closer to the bunny, she gently placed her hand on its back, moving very slowly. The bunny looked at her with a curious expression, simply allowing her to continue what she was doing.

Why did she feel more at ease with animals than with people? Throughout her life, she has only experienced fear when around others. Maybe she was born in the wrong body.

Lost in her own thoughts, she was surprised when her arm was suddenly pulled forward as the bunny jumped directly into the pond.

"What are you doing?" she yelled, confused by what just happened. However, she couldn't think for long after seeing the Bunny struggling to keep itself from drowning. So, without a moment's hesitation, she jumped right into the water, determined to save the bunny's life.

"Mmpph!"

The moment she entered the water, it felt as if tiny, sharp daggers were poking her all over her body. The water was freezing, and her instincts screamed at her to get out as fast as possible, but she wouldn't. As she searched for the bunny in the water, her body began to feel strange, and she started to feel dizzy. She struggled to focus and eventually found the white furball she was looking for.

Just before running out of air, she grabbed the bunny and fought her way to the surface. Teeth chattering and her body trembling violently, she managed to pull herself out of the water. But unlike the bright green grass that had been there before, the area around her was now covered in snow.

"Ack-ack!"

She coughed up some water, unable to prevent the bunny from wiggling free and running directly into the forest.

Trembling, she slowly got up and looked around. It seemed like the season had shifted. It was supposed to be mid-summer, but the ground and trees were covered in snow. She pinched herself to ensure she wasn't dreaming or hallucinating, but nothing changed.

Confused and scared, she realized she couldn't stay here. In her current condition, she might pass out from hyperthermia at any moment.

Slowly and steadily clinging to trees, she began to make her way out of the forest. As she walked, she noticed that her chest felt heavier and her balance was completely off. However, she forced herself to keep walking forward.

She didn't know how much time had passed, but in what seemed like hours to her, she finally reached the edge of the forest, only to find herself bewildered by her surroundings once again.

Everything around her had changed, from the buildings to the people. None of them looked familiar.

People looked at her with fear in their eyes. Some even turned away at just the sight of her. But she didn't care about them now. Her only thought was to find somewhere warm.

Her eyes grew heavy, and her knees felt like they were about to give out. In her hazy state, she was lucky to see the bright sign for a bookstore ahead of her.

Seeing this, she summoned the last of her strength to shove her way through the door, fighting against her body's impending collapse.

When she opened the door, she was greeted by the bright smile of a beautiful woman. She looked kind and safe, and…

"Welcome to—oh my! Hang in there, sweetie!" the woman yelled, her voice echoing in her ears before she passed out.

Chapter 2

"How is she a doctor?" a woman's voice asked, causing her to slowly wake up.

In the haze of waking, she could hear the woman's worried voice, puzzled about what was going on. The last thing she remembered was walking into the bookstore, and then everything went blank.

"She has a severe case of hypothermia, but thanks to you, she will live," a male voice said. "It was lucky that you found her when you did."

Oh, thank God! She was in such a poor state; I was worried the worst would happen.

"It truly is nothing more than a miracle that you did," the male doctor responded to her.

Unfortunately, she has no identification, so we'll have to wait until she wakes up to find out who she is. Hopefully, when she does, she can tell us how she ended up in such a condition.

Not understanding a word they were saying, she slowly began to open her eyes, seeing the outline of two people standing over her.

"Ugh, w-what happened?" she asked, her voice sounding scratchy and hoarse.

"Oh my! You're awake already!" the woman said, her bright orange hair catching her attention.

"Outstanding! Given your condition and size, you should have been unconscious for much longer than this," the doctor said, gazing at her with a curious look.

"W-where am I? What happened?"

Her mind was in disarray. Was she in a hospital?

Sweetie, don't you remember what happened to you?

The kind woman held her hand tightly, as if she were truly worried about her.

"You walked into my bookstore drenched from head to toe. I nearly had a heart attack when you suddenly collapsed like that. What was a poor girl like you doing in such a state?"

"… Poor girl?"

"Sweetie? Is there something wrong?" the woman asked her, noticing that she looked confused.

"What… what is this?" she asked herself, looking down to see that she was wearing a hospital gown.

How? Where? This had to be a dream. She must have passed out after leaving the water, right?

"Sweetie, are you okay?" the woman asked, glancing over at the doctor.

"Miss? My name is Dr. Kim; you're in the hospital. The woman next to me is Mrs. Dust. She brought you here after you collapsed. She saved your life. Do you remember what happened before you fell unconscious?"

"I… I fell in… in a pond," she said nervously. Every word that came out of her mouth felt strange.

"A pond! In this weather!" Mrs. Dust yelled, shocked.

The only pond near her store was located in the forest, close to the high school. That was at least a ten-minute walk away. How did such a small, frail-looking girl make her way to her store in this condition?

"Did someone push you into the pond?" Dr. Kim asked, trying to gather as much information as possible without overwhelming the girl.

"Did you jump in on purpose?"

"N-no, there was a bunny," she said nervously. Did she make them mad somehow? Why were they looking at her like this? She felt like she was going to throw up.

"I f-fell in the water… I jump in to… save it."

"Oh my! Sweetie, you had good intentions, but in this weather, you should have taken care of yourself."

Mrs. Dust gently held her hands. It was a miracle that such a pure girl like this survived.

"She is right," Dr. Kim said. "While what you did was noble, you risked your life. I will need to inform your parents or guardians of what happened. Could you please tell me your name and the best way to reach your family?"

"My name is… my name is…"

Huh? Why couldn't she say it? Her name was ...

"My name is…" She tried to say her name, but every time she did, she could feel her name becoming increasingly distant from her mind.

"Sweetie? Do you not remember your name?" Mrs. Dust asked, noticing the confused look on the girl's face. "Do you know where you are?"

"The hos-hospital?" she said, confused by the question. Her anxiety started to rise as she felt increasingly lost in the situation.

"No, sweetie, do you remember the name of this hospital? There is only one in this town," Mrs. Dust said, worried about the poor girl.

"It's uh… uh… what is it?" she asked, unable to answer her correctly.

"Doctor, what's going on? Why is she having difficulty remembering who she is and where she is?"

Mrs. Dust held her hand even tighter now.

"Hmm, it would seem that she has partial amnesia," Dr. Kim replied. "In times of great stress and life-threatening ordeals, it is not uncommon for victims to experience partial memory loss."

"Recent events, names, and even their location can be easily forgotten. Luckily, it's not life-threatening and can be easily cured by interacting with her family and loved ones. Miss, do you remember anything about your family or where to find them?"

"Family? I don't have one."

She remembered that she never had a family. She was raised in an orphanage, and there was never once a person she could call family in her entire life.

"Hmm, I'll have to post a bulletin about her. Her looks are unique, so if her family is looking for her, they will come for her."

"Let's see, blue eyes, white and blue hair, around, five feet tall."

"White and blue hair? No… my hair's brown," she said, looking at the doctor, confused by what he was talking about.

"Hmm, it seems she's a bit delirious from the cold. Miss, your hair is as white as snow with beautiful strands of blue inside it," the doctor said, holding up a mirror to show her reflection.

"What? What is this?" she asked, holding her hair in her hands. She was sure her hair wasn't this color. Did it somehow change because of the cold?

"Looks like someone dyed their hair before all of this," the doctor said, trying to make light of the issue. "For now, she'll have to stay at the hospital for at least a week before we can even consider discharging her."

"Um, doctor, may I talk with you alone for a moment?" Mrs. Dust asked. "Don't worry, sweetie. I'll be right back." Mrs. Dust gently released the girl's hands and walked out into the hall with the doctor so they couldn't hear their conversation.

As the days passed, she spent her time in the same hospital room where she had woken up. The nurses constantly took care of her, and she was undergoing treatment to improve her health.

After about a week, she was finally allowed to walk on her own, though it took her some time to adjust to everything. Everyone there was kind to her, and Mrs. Dust visited her regularly.

Despite their kindness, she worried it wouldn't last long. Since she had no family or friends, no one would be searching for her.

Like always, she was alone.

"Huh?"

Hearing the sound of a bubble being popped, she looked over to the door of her hospital room to see a young girl, no older than seventeen, with amber eyes and bright blonde hair, looking at her.

"So, you're the one she's been talking about for the past few days," the girl said to her. "I have to say, I'm not impressed."

"Hello? Who are you?" she asked, curious about who this girl was and why she seemed oddly familiar.

"Hmm, quite the docile one, aren't ya? I can see why she likes you. The name's Dust."

Dust? Wasn't that the last name of the woman who brought her here? Could she be related to Mrs. Dust?

"It's a pleasure to meet you." If she was related to Mrs. Dust, it would be best to be kind despite her outward demeanor. "I'm… uh…"

"It's fine. You don't have to say a word," Dust said, sitting in the chair beside the bed. "She said that you didn't remember your name. Don't sweat it."

Even after a week, she still hadn't remembered her name. Nurses tried to help her figure it out, but none of the names they suggested felt right. She felt empty, as if a part of her was missing.

"Hey, you don't have to get so down, I—"

"Oh my, it would seem that I'm a bit behind," Mrs. Dust said, entering the room. "Lily, I told you to wait, didn't I?"

"Mom! Don't use my real name!" Dust, or more accurately, Lily, complained to her mother.

Wait, mother? Although now that she thought about it, it made sense that they were related.

"I told you to call me Dust!"

"Lily, I don't care what your friends at school call you. I am your mother, and I will call you by the name I gave you. Now spit that gum out, young lady. This is a hospital. Show some respect."

"Yes, ma'am," Lily said, doing as she was told, completely ruining that relaxed girl vibe she had been trying to show the girl her mother had taken an interest in.

"I am sorry about that, sweetie. Lily's friends come up with the oddest-sounding nicknames. I believe that one of them is called Arid. But, no matter, kids will be kids. Before I get ahead of myself, I have some news to share with both of you."

"News?"

"Unfortunately, Dr. Kim says they couldn't determine your identity. They said that it's almost as if you appeared out of thin air. But they have made sure to send out bulletins to nearby towns in case you are a runaway or, heavens forbid, a victim of kidnapping."

"So, no one is coming for me."

Despite knowing that no one was coming for her, she clung to the small glimmer of hope that there was.

She could feel tears begin to well up in her eyes. Truly, nothing was different for her here or anywhere else.

"That's not true. I'm sure that wherever your family is right now, they are worried sick about you." Mrs. Dust wiped away her tears before holding her hands together.

"Though I think they would be more worried to find out you are homeless. Dr. Kim has informed me that within the next two weeks, your body should be fit enough to leave the hospital. Since you have nowhere to go, how would you like to come live with us?"

"Live with you?"

She was stunned by what she had just heard. She barely knew Mrs. Dust, but now she was being offered the chance to live with her. There was no way that someone could be this kind.

"Mom, what the heck are you talking about!" Lily yelled at her mother in disbelief. "Why on Earth would you offer to take in a girl that you met only a week ago?"

Mrs. Dust couldn't help but let out a small laugh at the girl's reactions. Of course, it made no sense for her to offer her home to a stranger, but this girl was different; she could feel it. She wasn't rude, whiny, or cunning; she was just a lost girl with nowhere to go.

How could she possibly leave a girl like this on her own? The world was a scary place, and she feared that, if left alone, this poor girl could be harmed. She refused to turn away someone in need. It was something her husband would do if he were still alive.

"I... I..."

"Sweetie, I'm not trying to force you to do something you don't want to do," Mrs. Dust said, gently looking at her. "Please allow me, no, allow us to help you."

"Don't I get a say in this?" Lily looked at her mother with a confused glare.

Mrs. Dust felt sorry for the girl, but there was no way she could let a stranger live in her home. But this girl would have to survive on the streets if she didn't. There was no way she could force a girl this frail-looking out on her own. Despite her reluctance, it was clear that Lily had a kind heart, just like her mother.

"Lily, please don't say that you don't want to help her. I know I raised you better than to turn your back on those in need."

"Fine, but she better not touch any of my clothes," Lily said, turning away so they wouldn't see her start to blush. "You have to buy her clothes of her own."

"That can be arranged," Mrs. Dust said, happy that her daughter was kind enough to insist on buying this girl new clothes instead of for herself.

"As I said, this is a decision that you don't need to force yourself to answer. I could even recommend a nice shelter for young girls if you'd like. It's a bit strict with rules, but the girls there are well-fed, clothed, and cared for. I want to make sure that you're safe."

Safe? Never before had anyone asked her what she wanted or cared for her like this. People usually expected her to obey their commands without question. There was no true concern or worry in any of their requests. What should she do? Should she go with them? Could she find happiness if she did?

Chapter 3

"A-are you sure I won't be a bother?" she asked, hoping this wasn't a cruel trick.

"Sweetie, you could never be a bother," Mrs. Dust told her. This girl looked like she had been through far too much heartache for her age. What she needed right now was love and affection.

"Yeah, don't sweat it," Lily said to her. "You did nothing wrong to think you would be a bother. Now stop hesitating and just say yes already."

"I... I would like that very much," she said, feeling a sense of warmth from their smiles.

Before all of this, she expected her life to be filled with suffering. It felt unreal that she had met people this kind to her.

"You won't regret this!"

In a spur-of-the-moment move, Mrs. Dust hugged her, pulling Lily in.

"Um, mom, I think we need to discuss the elephant in the room before we do anything else," Lily said.

While she was okay with allowing this girl to live with them and thought it would be cool to have a little sister, there was a significant problem: "She needs a name."

"Oh my! How could I forget!" Mrs. Dust gasped.

"A name?"

She had been trying to figure out her name for the past week. Maybe it would be better to accept a new one than to try to remember the one she had lost.

"Since you currently don't remember your name, I think it would be best if we came up with a new one. It is only temporary, of course, but what do you think? Do you have anything in mind?"

"N-no I don't," she said, unable to think of one, fearing that if she could come up with a name, it would slip away from her just as her original name had.

"That's alright. If it isn't too forward of me, I do have a suggestion, if that's alright with you. I was thinking that you could be called Snow. Since we found you on quite a snowy day, and since your hair is a beautiful white and blue. I thought it would be fitting, or am I being insensitive?"

"Snow?"

The name rolled off her tongue as if it weren't the first time she had been called by this name. "I love it," Snow said to her, accepting the name given to her. It felt natural, and she loved it even more since it was a name Mrs. Dust had thought up for her. There was no way that she wouldn't accept it.

"Thank you!" Mrs. Dust yelled, hugging her some more.

Lily couldn't help but think that this was a bit cringe, but she also couldn't help but feel happy for Snow.

"Now, all we need to do is have you sign some paperwork."

"Paperwork?" Snow asked, confused as to why she was being asked that.

"One is to legalize your name. And the other is your agreement to live with us. Please stay here while I go get the paperwork!"

Before Snow could have a second more to think, Mrs. Dust ran straight out of the room.

"Sorry about that," Lily said to Snow. "My mother can be a bit over-eager sometimes. It looks like she likes you, and you seem like a good enough kid. If you need anything, just let me know, and I'll do my best to help.

"Thank you… Dust?" Snow said, unsure if she could call her that or Lily.

"It's fine. You can call me Lily. Only my friends call me Dust."

"Friends…"

Did she ever have friends before? Her memories of the past were vague, almost as if they were a dream.

"No, no, no, it's not like that!" Lily yelled, worried she had upset Snow. "It's just a silly nickname, that's all. There's nothing more to it. I'm trying to say that you don't need to force yourself to call me that. I… I'd prefer if you called me Lily."

"You're not as mean as you look," Snow said, letting out a small laugh. Lily may have seemed calm and composed when she first saw her, but Snow could tell she was actually quite cute.

"Hey, don't laugh!" Lily blushed, trying to hide her embarrassment. "Don't think that I'll be this nice when you move in! And don't expect to share a room with me! You're getting your own!"

Snow could only smile back at her. Lily was just like her mother, filled with kindness. If only she had met them earlier, maybe her life would have been different, and she wouldn't have found herself in this situation.

"Oh my, it looks like you two are getting along," Mrs. Dust said, standing in the doorway with a bright smile. Snow had noticed her there already but said nothing. It was fun watching Lily get embarrassed like this.

"What do you mean, get along? I'm only going to tolerate her because you asked. Don't expect me to help her that much, okay?"

"Of course," her mother said, teasing her and knowing her daughter's true thoughts. "Although I expect you to help with the preparations before she moves in."

"Fine, whatever. Can we just get this over with already? Can't you see that she's tired?"

"You're right. I was being insensitive; she does look quite tired. I brought the paperwork. Once you sign, your name will legally become Snow Dust. I wasn't sure what last name to give you, but I hope you wouldn't mind taking mine."

"I would love to," Snow said, signing the papers without hesitation. There was no way that she could have dreamed of something like this before.

"Welcome to our family," Mrs. Dust said, hugging the girl again. She promised herself that this girl would receive all the love she deserved.

Chapter 4

-Two Weeks Later-

"How do they fit, sweetie?" Mrs. Dust asked Snow, who was doing her best to put on the clothes given to her, as they were clearly way too big for her.

"They f-feel alright," Snow said, tugging at her clothes.

"There's no need to force yourself to like them. These are Lily's old clothes. She wore those when she was a freshman in high school. She's grown quite tall since then, even though you two are roughly the same age according to the doctor. It's a wonder why you're so small."

"She's just too big…"

"It's okay, sweetie. There's no need to feel self-conscious about that. You are perfect just the way you are," Mrs. Dust said, trying to comfort her.

"Mom, the car is ready!" Lily said, walking into the room after warming up the car to make sure Snow wouldn't get sick. "Mom, are you teasing her again?"

Lily knew how her mother could be and that she had to protect Snow from her over-possessiveness.

"Nonsense, sweetie, now come along; it's time for us to get you some new clothes! I know you look great in whatever you decide to wear."

"T-thank you, Mrs. Dust," Snow said back to her, grateful for everything she had done for her.

"Sweetie, you don't have to keep calling me Mrs. Dust. You can call me by my name, Autumn. Or, if you're willing to… no, that's silly of me…"

"Now let's get going!" she eagerly said, leading the two girls to the car before driving them to the best clothing store she knew: Lucy's.

She had been trying to get Lily to come here for years, but she always complained that the clothes were too girly. With Snow, she could finally have some fun.

"Welcome to Lucy's! My name is Rae. I am here to help you with anything you need."

A girl no taller than Snow with black hair approached them, greeting them warmly.

"Thank you. Today, we need to buy clothes for this one right here," Autumn said, proudly showing Snow to Rae. "Since we're between winter and spring, I think it would be best to get her both heavy and light clothes."

"Splendid idea," Rae replied, happy to see actual customers. Most girls who come here usually browse. She could finally show off her talent and was given a fine canvas to work on.

"We have just started laying out our spring clothing line, and the winter clothing line is currently on sale."

"Oh, do you perhaps have any deals?" Autumn asked, trying not to embarrass Snow.

"We do! I'll take her to an empty dressing room to get her properly measured. Come along, dear."

Rae gently took Snow's hand and led her to the changing room. For the next hour, Snow tried on outfit after outfit while others admired her. From pants to shorts, skirts, and dresses, she tried everything—cute tops, blouses, coats, and hats. There was nothing she didn't try on.

"Marvelous," Rae said, knowing Snow would be the perfect model for her. Her beauty was as striking as Rae's, and she was confident she could create some stunning twin outfits with her. "Do you know what you'll be buying today?"

"Of course, we'll take it all," Lily said, proud to see Snow in such lovely clothes. There was no way her mother wouldn't buy everything Snow wore.

"A-all of it?"

Rae was stunned by what she just heard. That was several hundred dollars worth of clothes. This had to be a joke.

"My daughter is right," Autumn said, wondering if this was enough. Still, she knew it was probably best to stop here. Snow looked tired and anxious. She was still recovering, so it was best not to push her too hard.

"..."

Snow nervously tugged at Autumn's sleeve. While she was glad they were willing to do this for her, she didn't need all of this.

"...What I mean to say is that we'll take half."

"Alright, and if you could please pay here."

Rae led them to the cash register, allowing Autumn to pay for half of what Snow tried on.

"Wonderful! Thank you for your purchase!"

"Thank you for your help. We will come back again," Autumn said, helping Snow out of the store. Lily followed behind them, carrying the clothes they had purchased.

"That was definitely fun. What would you like to do next? Should we head home or grab something to eat first?"

"Um, I could go for something to eat," Snow responded.

She had been living on hospital food for a while and wanted to try something different. Plus, this would give her a chance to explore more of this strange place.

As they left the hospital, Snow realized they were no longer in the same spot. The streets and stores looked different. It was as if she had entered a different world.

"Yeah, I'm starving," Lily said with a smile. "I need to hit my daily calorie goal, or I won't be able to function properly. I want to be in top shape for track season."

"Alright, how about sushi? I recently found a really nice place. Are you girls okay with that?"

"I g-guess," Snow said. She'd never tried sushi before, but she was open to it.

"Don't worry, you'll love it!" Lily said, giving her a quick pat on the back, already eager to eat.

"Then sushi it is!" Autumn cheered, starting the car and driving off.

Luckily, they didn't have to go far; the drive took only a few minutes, and once they arrived, Autumn and

Lily wasted no time bringing Snow inside so she wouldn't be cold.

"Welcome! Would you like a booth or a table?" a girl with red wavy hair asked them as they entered.

The atmosphere of the restaurant felt warm despite being almost empty, and it was clear that the servers were very friendly as well.

"We would like a booth, please," Autumn said, knowing it would be more comfortable for Snow.

"Alrighty then, come this way," the girl responded, leading them to a nearby booth. "My name is Ember, and if you need anything, don't hesitate to ask. Your menus are at your table, and I will come back in a few minutes to take your order."

"Wow… that's Ember?" Lily whispered, but Autumn and Snow still heard her.

"Do you know her?"

"Not exactly, but some pretty nasty rumors have been going around about her. They say she was a serious bully who hurt anyone who crossed her. No one could stop her. Not even the teachers would interfere."

"But those are just rumors, right?" Autumn asked, hoping her daughter would know how to tell the difference between truth and gossip.

"Yeah, but there are several hate channels online dedicated to her, so some of it must be true."

"Y-you shouldn't believe sites like that," Snow warned her.

"She's right," Autumn said back to her, glad to see that Snow wouldn't be swayed by rumors. "Rumors can't be trusted. You can only trust things you have seen for yourself or heard from those you trust."

"I'm just saying these rumors couldn't have started from nothing. There has to be some truth to them. Just because she looks nice right now doesn't mean she is a good person."

Ember stood in front of their table, holding a tray of water. It was clear she had heard everything Lily said about her.

"…I'm sorry. If you would like another server, I can—"

"I would like a sa-sashimi plate, please," Snow said softly, grabbing her hand before Ember could run off. "And I would like you to serve it."

"Th-that's one sashimi," Ember said, feeling relieved that another person didn't drive her away.

Things had been difficult since "that" day, but she was trying to move past it, and kindness like this girl's went a long way.

"And I would like a uramaki set," Autumn said, glad to see what Snow did for the young girl. "As for my rude daughter, she can have a spicy tuna roll and add a side of wasabi."

"Yes, ma'am, your order will be out shortly!" Ember replied happily as she headed to the back.

"Mom, you know I don't like wasabi. It's too spicy," Lily complained, fidgeting in her seat.

"I don't care. You need to learn your lesson and stop listening to rumors. You hurt that poor girl's feelings, and you will apologize when she gets back, and I expect you'll use all of your allowance as a tip.

"What! That's not fair!"

"Either you apologize to her and give her a more than generous tip, or you won't get your allowance for the next year. Do I make myself clear?"

Autumn loved Lily with all her heart, but there were many times when she acted too rashly. She needed to learn her lesson.

"Fine," Lily said, defeated by her mother again.

Snow giggled, watching the mother-daughter duo argue. She had never had a family before, so this was a new and enjoyable experience for her.

"What are you laughing at?" Lily asked, smiling at her, realizing that she was being foolish. It wasn't right for her to believe rumors, and she looked foolish in front of Snow. "I'm going to put some wasabi on your food as punishment."

"You will do no such thing," Autumn responded to her daughter with a smile.

"You're the same as always, Autumn," a woman wearing a rainbow flag pin on her shirt said, sitting at the table next to their booth. Her bright blonde hair stood out the most among everyone else.

"Tanya, is that you? Oh my god, I haven't seen you in ages; how have you been?" Autumn asked, glad to see her friend after such a long time.

"I've been good," the woman replied. "It's been a while since I last saw you. And oh my, is that Lily? Do you remember me?"

"Auntie Tanya?" Lily said, surprised to see her again after all this time.

"Bravo, you remembered! Though Autumn, I could have sworn that Lily was your only daughter. Who might this cute young lady be?"

"I… I'm Snow," she said shyly, looking at the confident woman.

"She was recently temporarily adopted into our family," Autumn explained, clarifying who Snow was.

"Snow has amnesia. She doesn't remember who she was before I found her, and I decided to take care of her until she does."

"That is just like you," Tanya said, recalling when Autumn met her future husband back in high school. But she knew better than to dig up old wounds.

"Alright, I'm back with your—mom! What are you doing here?" Ember yelled, noticing her mother at her workplace.

"Can't a mother see her daughter at work?" Tanya teased her. "What are you worried I might embarrass you?"

"Ugh! Do whatever you want. I'll get your usual order," she said before walking into the back again.

"Always one to never take things easy. I always find it interesting to see how much of myself is in her," Tanya said proudly, looking at Ember. "It's somewhat hard having to worry about her all the time, but my job is so much more than I care about one single child. My job makes me worry about others as well."

"Whatever do you mean?" Autumn asked curiously, wondering what her friend was trying to imply.

Chapter 5

"Is this young lady enrolled in school yet?" Tanya asked Autumn, noticing that the two girls were too busy with their food to hear them talking.

"Not yet; today, she was just released from the hospital. I was planning to consider enrolling her later, in about a month or so, to give her time to settle in. I need to figure out which school would be the best fit for her," Autumn told her friend.

"I would like to send her to the same school as Lily, but that is a private school and quite expensive. The only reason Lily is able to go there is because of her athletic scholarships."

"If you're having such a hard time figuring it out, why not just send her to Silver Valley High? It's a public school, and it's near your bookstore, so if anything happens, you can get there relatively quickly. And as the principal, I can guarantee her safety. My daughter also goes there, and they'll be in the same grade, so I could ask her and her friends to look out for her."

"Would you permit that? It's already past the halfway point of the school year. Won't there be rumors spreading around?"

Autumn was worried. Snow had just physically recovered, and her mental state was fragile. She feared Snow would be bullied.

"It'll be fine," Tanya said, reassuring her. "And, if it helps, I can inform the teachers that she has a weak constitution, and they should try to help her avoid stressful situations."

"That would be amazing, but why? Why go this far for us?"

"It's simple," Tanya said, looking over at Snow, who struggled to use her chopsticks. "It's because I love helping young people grow. It's the main reason I became an educator and a principal. I want to help them grow up in a safe and happy environment."

"Hmm. While I would love to accept your offer, that choice is not mine to make; it's hers," Autumn said, looking over at Snow, who had finally managed to grab her sashimi with her chopsticks but dropped it again when she noticed they were talking about her.

"Snow, how do you feel about going to school?"

"S-school?"

Snow didn't have many fond memories of her time in school. She was a social outcast, always keeping to herself. She never fit in and was often bullied. School wasn't a pleasant experience for her.

"I don't know."

If she went to school, she would be alone again, and she didn't want to be alone. She nervously picked at her food, unable to make a choice.

"Snow, you don't have to go to school if you don't want to," Tanya said, seeing that Snow was worried about upsetting her. "But I would love it if you did. School is a place where you get to learn and grow with your peers. You can learn many things and make lifelong friends. Doesn't that sound nice?"

"But… but no one would want to be friends with me."

Snow recalled the trauma of having "friends" and then being abandoned by them when times got tough. She didn't want to go through that again.

"Sweetie, why would you say that?" Autumn put her arm around the poor girl, holding her close to comfort her.

Whatever she went through before losing her memories must be haunting her. Autumn wanted nothing more than to protect this small and innocent child. "There would be many who would be glad if you became their friend."

"She's right," Lily said to her. "It would be hard for anyone to hate you. Our security is top-notch to protect all of our students.

"But I…"

"You'll love it. The teachers are nice, too."

"But I..."

"Mom, what are you doing?" Ember asked, returning with Tanya's usual order, surprised to see that these two adults and an older girl had this one girl on the verge of tears.

"Ember, we were just talking about enrolling her in your school. Doesn't that sound wonderful?"

Tanya was happy that her daughter had returned, recognizing this as the perfect opportunity for the two of them to start forming a connection.

"It sounds like you're being a noisy busybody again." Ember grabbed Snow's hand, pulling her out of the booth. "Come on, I'll take you to a place where you can calm down."

"Okay…"

Snow felt grateful. She didn't know how to respond when they treated her so kindly. It was overwhelming.

"I…"

"It's all right, you don't have to say a thing," Ember reassured her. "And you three can stay here," she added, leading Snow to the back break room where she could finally find some peace.

"I'm sorry you had to deal with that. I know what it's like to feel overwhelmed. I've had many bad days where I couldn't handle it and broke down."

"How did you handle it?" Snow asked, wondering how she could overcome this anxiety consuming her.

"I couldn't. At least I couldn't by myself, I had my friends to help me overcome it. I know you heard some rumors from the girl you were sitting with, and some of them are true. I've made many mistakes that will always haunt me, but thanks to my friends, I don't have to bear them alone. Each of them has a unique way of making me feel like I belong."

"Rae is always thinking about fashion. So much so that every activity she leads has us dressing up in one way or another. Sometimes, it can be a bit much, but no one ever says that to her."

Diana loves baking. She's always bringing sweets to class and sharing them with everyone. She enjoys seeing her friends smile. However, sometimes she can take things too far. Once, she made a cake so tall that when the judges were inspecting it, it toppled onto them.

"Th-that's hilarious," Snow said, laughing as she started to calm down thanks to Ember.

"Then there's Allison. Her family runs a small knick-knack shop. She is honest and hardworking to a fault. She's always there to stand up for others, even when sometimes they don't deserve it," Ember said, her tone sounding depressed for a second. "She is a bit dense when it comes to love, but she'll always tell the truth, especially when you need to hear it."

"And don't get me started on Alice. She's as loud as they come, always causing trouble and never sitting still. But when you need to blow off some steam, she's always there to help. She's a bit overeager at times, but I can't say I find that a problem.

"And then there's Faye; she's a timid girl. Despite her shyness, she always does her best in everything she does. She loves animals and never backs down. She's one of the bravest girls I know."

"Your friends sound amazing," Snow told her, wishing she could meet them.

"There is one other friend, but she… she's far away right now."

A depressed tone came from her as she mentioned this friend.

"It's okay, you don't have to talk about it if y-you don't want to," Snow said, placing her hand on Ember's."

"Thanks. My friends are great, and I think they would like you if you met them. Most students at Silver Valley High are nice. There are many oddballs, but those people are just unique. I hope this doesn't stress you out, but you should attend Silver Valley High School. I think that you'll like it."

"I think that I would like that."

Snow saw that Ember was unlike anyone she had known before. She was kind and gentle; she was a true friend, or at least that was what Snow hoped she could be.

"Do you think we can stay here a bit longer?"

"Sure, no problem," Ember replied.

Snow was unaware of the rumors circulating about her. She truly was a kind-hearted girl who attracted others easily. Although Ember worried about what Snow might think if she found out the truth, she couldn't dwell on it; she simply couldn't.

"Are you all right?" Snow asked, noticing Ember's expression darken.

"I'm fine. I was thinking that I should introduce you to Faye once you enroll. She works at an animal shelter and is the president of the pet welfare club. Pets are a great way to help you relax and calm down when you become too stressed or start having a panic attack. I'm sure that being near her would help a lot."

"Thanks."

Snow felt happy that Ember was thinking of her even though they had just met today. Not everyone was as bad as she had thought. Maybe there are other people out there filled with kindness like her.

"Ember?" Tanya asked, knocking on the door from the other side. "Are you alright? Your boss says that he needs you out here to take orders."

"I'm coming." Ember rose to her feet, glad she had spent this time with Snow. "I hope I'll see you around," she said, opening the door to reveal everyone waiting for them.

"Hey, sorry about before," Lily said, apologizing to Ember as she left the room. "And thanks for…"

"Don't mention it," Ember said, accepting the apology before walking away.

"Snow, sweetie, are you all right?" Autumn asked, worried. She didn't notice the signs that they were overwhelming her, and she almost brought the poor girl to tears.

"I'm fine," Snow told them, pleased they cared about her. "Um, if it isn't too m-much to ask, I would like to attend Silver Valley High School."

"Really?"

Autumn was surprised that Snow was brave enough to ask her for that. This was the first thing that she had requested from her. There was no way that she could deny her.

"Y-yes. I think… no, I want to go to school and make some friends."

Chapter 6

A month and a half had passed since Snow began living with Autumn and Lily. During this time, she had adjusted to her new life with them. Snow even helped out at the bookstore to prove her worth, organizing books and watching Autumn interact with customers.

It was enjoyable, and she was having a great time. However, the one thing she couldn't get used to was their kindness. Snow had never experienced the warmth of a family and worried that it could disappear at any moment.

She just had to hope that her life would keep being like this. She wanted to continue having a family.

The shop's door made a small chime as it opened, and a new customer entered. To Snow's surprise, it was none other than Ember.

During this month and a half, Ember had been coming by frequently, gradually becoming close friends with Snow.

Autumn greeted her warmly, saying, "Ember, you're here early, dear. Shouldn't you still be in class?"

"I have a free period, so my mom asked me to come by early and bring Snow down," Ember said, giving Snow a slight wave as she watched her stack a few books.

Snow returned the wave with a weak smile.

"That would be lovely," Autumn happily responded, remembering that today was the day Snow would check out the school before being officially enrolled.

"Snow, come along, let's get you ready."

"I can do it myself," Snow said, blushing. She didn't want to be treated like a child, but she found it hard to refuse Autumn's kindness.

"I know you can, sweetie, but just to be safe. You've only recently recovered, and your body may still be frail. I don't want to take any risks that could cause you to get sick again."

"I'm sorry about that," Snow said to Ember as they left the bookstore, walking towards the school.

"It's fine. My mom can be like that sometimes, too," Ember said, knowing all too well what it was like to have an overbearing mother. "Though it's nice, right? Knowing that they care so much about you. Even if you do something that you can never undo…"

Ember paused for a second, sparking Snow's curiosity about what she was thinking, but she felt it wasn't her place to ask.

"It's great to have a family, so don't take them for granted. You never know how much they mean to you until they're gone."

"Y-yeah, you're right," Snow said to her, knowing that without Autumn, she might have been dead right now. "Family is great."

If only she could be an actual member of their family.

"Snow, look, we're here." Ember grabbed Snow's hand, guiding her toward the building before them.

The school wasn't far from the bookstore, so the few-minute commute would be easy. And if anything happened to her, Autumn could get there right away.

"Welcome to Silver Valley High."

"Wow, it's amazing!"

Snow couldn't believe her eyes. Just by entering the school, she could tell what a large and impressive place it was. Everything felt surreal. When they arrived, several students looked their way, but Ember blocked their gaze.

"Right now, we are in the main hall, and over here, we have the trophy case filled with some of the trophies that other students have won over the years. And over here is…"

"Psst! Psst!"

Snow looked over and saw a short, brown-haired student trying to catch her attention. The girl said nothing, but Snow could see her mouth form the letters R-U-N.

Run? Why would she run?

"Snow, are you listening?" Ember asked, grabbing Snow's attention once more.

"S-sorry," Snow said, feeling bad for turning away while Ember was talking.

"There's no need to feel sorry. Come on, there's a lot more to see." Ember saw what that one girl tried to do and didn't want Snow to be influenced by the nasty rumors circulating about her.

"The principal's office, where my mom works, is over here, and next to it is where my aunt, the vice-principal, works. It would be best not to linger in her office for too long; she is quite the stickler for the rules.

Ember led Snow around the school for the next hour, silently watching the classes they saw. Each one looked like a lot of fun, with happy students and teachers. This was unusual when she went to school, as it was rare to see kids who genuinely wanted to learn and enjoy class.

"And with that, classes are done for the day," Ember happily said, hearing the end of the school day. "How about we check out some clubs? Do you have anything in mind, or would you like me to choose?"

"C-can we go to your club?"

Snow was curious to see what club Ember was in. She had never been in a club before and thought they could be fun.

"My club?"

"Yeah. What is your club?" Snow asked again, hoping she wasn't being too bold. If she had to join a club, she wouldn't mind being part of one with someone like Ember.

"Sure, we can check out my club," Ember said, happy to see that Snow was taking an interest in her.

"I'm in a band as well as the cooking club. Would you like to see where we practice?"

"Y-yeah," Snow smiled, seeing how happy Ember was.

"Come on, let's go!"

Ember eagerly grabbed Snow's hand and led her to the band room. She was unaware that Snow's face was turning beet red from embarrassment. Snow still wasn't used to holding hands with other girls, especially those as pretty as Ember.

"Currently, no one is here since we have to schedule in advance when we want to practice, but I like coming here to relax. It gets me away from everyone else, and that's more than enough."

"W-what do you play?" Snow was curious to see which one of the many instruments surrounding them Ember played.

"Me? I don't play an instrument. I'm the singer."

"You can sing?" Snow asked, curious about what she sounded like.

"Yeah, and I'm actually pretty good… or at least that's what the other girls tell me." Ember blushed, not understanding why. "Next time the band is together, we can play something for you."

"I would like that," Snow said, somewhat excited to hear Ember sing.

"Well, gosh dang, to think that I would be able to see this," a blonde-haired girl said, walking into the room.

"Allison, what are you doing here?" Ember asked her, curious as to why her friend was here when they didn't have practice until later this week.

"I came to replace the strings on my bass; it was starting to get plum out of tune," Allison replied, looking straight at Snow. Snow was starting to get a tad bit nervous, seeing a girl who was taller than Lily tower above her. "What about you?"

"Allison, this is Snow; remember the girl I told you about before?"

"I do remember quite well," Allison said, holding out her hand. "It's mighty fine to meet you, Snow; I'm Allison."

"I-I'm Snow," she said, introducing herself, slowly taking Allison's hand as she received a firm handshake.

"Quite the tiny one, ain't ya? You're just as small as Rae. I know she'll be dying to get along with you."

"Y-yes?" Snow responded nervously, trying to figure out what she should say to the tall girl.

"Allison…"

'Sorry, sorry," Allison said, noticing Snow's face turn beet red. This tiny little lady really did have a problem with receiving attention. She would have to help this poor girl.

"As I said, I'm just here to replace the strings on my bass, though I could leave and give you two a bit more alone time if you want?"

"Allison, please don't joke around like that! Just look at her! Her face is beat red!"

"…"

Snow couldn't help but feel embarrassed. There was no way that someone as amazing as Ember could ever think about her in that way.

Wait!

What was she thinking? No… even considering something like this was something she should never do.

"All right, I was just kidding. I'm sorry," Allison said, knowing that it was only proper for her to apologize once more.

"It's okay," Snow tried to reassure her that she did nothing wrong. She found talking to someone who could joke casually around her pleasant. She had never had a person act like that around her before; it felt amazing.

"Snow, even if you say it's fine and even though Allison holds no ill will towards you, you need to express yourself to make sure that people understand you," Ember said, remembering what she went through when all the rumors began.

"O-okay," Snow blushed, happy that Ember cared for her. She truly was a nice person. To think that there were people who would spread nasty rumors about her.

"Good." Ember was glad that Snow was taking her advice to heart. "Would you like to go explore some more?"

"Yes." Snow was happy to meet Allison, but she just wanted to spend her time near Ember.

"Hey, don't let me get in the way of your bonding," Allison said, seeing that it would be best to let these two get close for now. "Ya'll go have some fun."

Chapter 7

"I was thinking that we could head down to the cooking club next," Ember said, eager to show Snow some of her cooking skills.

"O-okay, let's—"

"Ember, you aren't causing trouble again, are you?" a woman with dark black hair asked, walking up behind them.

"Aunt Adrienne, what are you doing here?" Ember asked, nervous to see her aunt of all people.

"I'm here to make sure that students either participate in their extracurricular activities or go home. What are you doing right now?"

"I'm showing Snow around the school. Mom asked me to."

"H-hi, I'm Snow," she said, giving a slight wave while trying to avoid the stern gaze directed at her.

"Hmm, Snow… ah, you must be the student starting classes next week. Snow Dust, if I'm not mistaken. My sister must have convinced you to come here. She's always been good at taking in strays."

As Adrienne mentioned that Snow noticed her eyes drifting over to Ember. Was something happening between the two of them?

"I'm not here because of her," Snow said, not liking the way this woman was looking at Ember. "I'm here for Ember."

"Hmm, if that's the case, then you could have chosen a different reason," Adrienne said to Snow, who couldn't understand why Ember's aunt would act like this around here. Ember said that she was a stickler for the rules, but by the looks of it, she didn't seem to like Ember.

"Hmm?"

"Choosing to go to school because of a single person you don't even know is never a wise choice. Once you are fully enrolled and have started classes, it's best to focus on your studies. Having friends is nice, but that can come later. What matters most is learning. Some girls are better suited to show you around than she is. Allow me to schedule a—"

"No," Snow said firmly, not wanting to be near anyone besides Ember.

"I'm sorry, but I could have sworn that you said no to me."

Adrienne looked surprised. She did not expect that such a weak and timid girl would deny her so adamantly.

"No. I don't want anyone but her," Snow said, doing her best not to stutter and to sound strong, but she could already feel like she was about to collapse.

"Have you not heard the rumors surrounding her? Aren't you curious about what you will learn about her?"

"No, and I don't care; E-Ember is a nice person, and she… and sh…."

Snow started to feel lightheaded, losing the strength in her legs.

"Don't worry, I'm here," Ember said, catching Snow so she wouldn't fall. "Aunt, please, this is enough. We can talk about this at home."

"As I said before, for a girl this weak and frail, there are those better suited for her to be around. After everything that has happened, do you truly wish to gain another burden?"

Adrienne's words were directed at Ember like a cold blade. Snow could feel her grip loosen for a second. Snow didn't quite understand what she was talking about, but she couldn't help but think that there was some hidden meaning behind her words.

"It's fine. I can handle it," Ember said to her. "I will definitely be someone she can trust."

"Then you'd best work hard; someone with your reputation will have to. As for you, Miss Dust, I look forward to seeing you on Monday with your guardian to discuss further details. For now, you'd best head to the nurse's office. It would seem that you need some rest."

"I'll make sure she gets there."

Ember and Snow watched Adrienne walk away, leaving a distasteful aura in the air.

"Ember, are you okay?" Snow asked, feeling mentally drained after standing up to Adrienne.

"I'm fine, what about you? How are you feeling?" Ember supported Snow in her arms, hoping that she wouldn't collapse. The color had drained from her face, and her entire body was trembling.

"I… I would like to sit down."

Her legs felt like jelly. If she had to stand any longer, then Ember might as well become her new legs.

"Alright, let's do that," Ember said, leading her over to a bench and allowing Snow to sit down. "Stay right here for a second; I'm going to run down the hall and get you a drink from the vending machines."

"Wait, you don't have to…"

Before Snow could tell her no, Ember was already making her way down the hall, leaving her alone as other students stared at her, making her feel nervous.

Luckily for her, Ember was quick and returned to Snow in a few minutes.

"Here, this should help," Ember said, handing Snow a bottle of iced tea.

"T-thank you."

Snow eagerly accepted the drink given to her. The cold drink was exactly what she needed to relax. She had stressed herself out by standing up to Adrienne, and while she didn't regret it, she knew that it would be best not to push herself like that again.

"Um, Ember, about what the vice-principal…"

"Oh, that, well, it wasn't as big as you might have thought it was."

Ember understood why Snow was confused, realizing it was better that she learned now than later.

My aunt has a strict way of speaking. Mom says she got it from Grandma. Early on, she was right when she told you that there were girls who were better suited to show you around than I was. The school has students who assist with the sick and elderly. They are more suited to helping those with weak health, like yourself. She was only trying to help you.

"And the rumors?"

Snow didn't want to know about the rumors surrounding Ember, but it didn't seem like she could avoid them while attending this school. She knew it was for the best if she heard about them from Ember herself.

"It looks like I have no other choice now," Ember sighed, realizing she had to tell Snow.

"It all started—"

"My, my, my, the rumors are true," a pale brown-haired girl said, walking over to them, interrupting Ember before she could tell Snow anything. "It would seem that Ember is hanging around someone new."

"Hmm? Who are you?" Snow asked, confused, who this girl was.

"Oh my, your voice is amazing. I would love to introduce myself, but it seems that you have something behind your ear," the girl said, moving her hand behind Snow's ear and pulling out a white rose, much to her surprise.

"Here, for the nice young lady."

The girl graciously held out the rose, and Snow took it, unable to keep herself from blushing.

"Estella, what are you doing here?" Ember asked, worried that Estella, of all people, had to come here.

"You make it sound like I can't be here," Estella said, holding her head high. "Why wouldn't I take the chance to introduce myself to a soon-to-be fan? There are rumors all around about how Ember is walking around the school with a white-haired girl. So there was no way that I wouldn't be interested."

"Estella, I'm just trying to show her around the school. Snow is very shy, so I would prefer it if you left us alone for now."

"Snow, that's a very pretty name," Estella said, pulling out a blue rose and handing it to Snow, who couldn't help but accept it.

"I'm n-not pretty…"

Snow was nervous talking to Estella, but honestly, she was also interested in her. She had never known a magician before, so she couldn't help but stare.

"Ah, you must be right. Such a beauty like you can't be just pretty; your looks are of an angel that has descended from the heavens," Estella said, causing Snow to blush even more and making her heart race.

"I…" Snow looked away in embarrassment, unable to bear Estella's sweet words any longer.

"Estella, please, that's enough," Ember said, worried for Snow's health.

"Alright, if you insist," Estella agreed, seeing that Snow's face was beat red. "Here, have one of these," she said, handing Snow a chocolate bar.

"T-thank you," Snow said, taking the chocolate bar and noticing how Estella's attitude had changed.

"No problem. I'm Estella, and you?" Estella asked Snow, properly introducing herself.

"I'm Snow."

"It's a pleasure. Are you feeling alright?" Estella asked, noticing that this girl was experiencing anemia.

"Yes," Snow said, a little embarrassed that someone else was already caring about her.

"That's good. I'm sorry if I excited you too much before; being a magician means putting on an act, so I need to make sure that people know who I am. Though I wasn't lying when I said you were as cute as an angel. Perhaps you could become my assistant."

"Estella," Ember said firmly, noticing that Estella was once again trying to recruit an assistant for her show. She was always like this, finding a girl who catches her eye and then attempting to get them to be her assistant. However, so far, it's never worked.

"Fine, I'll give up… for now."

"Snow, this is Estella; she's… she's a friend."

"Hey, don't think I didn't hear that pause when you said that," Estella said, smiling at Ember.

"Estella helped me out a while back when things weren't looking too good for me. I owe her a lot."

"For the last time, I do not require you to owe me anything.'

"But I insist."

"Hmph!"

Snow couldn't help but giggle, seeing how close they were.

"Anyway, Ember, you should be careful. Those rumors are still going around," Estella said, well aware of why the rumors existed, but she knew better than to believe them.

"Rumors?" Snow asked, recalling that Ember was about to tell her, but couldn't because of Estella's arrival.

"Snow, about those rumors there—"

"They're all fake," Estella interjected. "Not too long ago, something bad happened to her. Many people blamed her for what transpired and started to shun her, but the truth is she did nothing wrong."

"Estella, you don't have—"

"Yes, yes, you don't have to thank me. You just need to ignore them."

"It's okay," Snow assured her, recognizing that Estella was helping Ember. "You don't need to say it until you want to."

"Thank you."

"And where's my thanks?" Estella asked, a smile on her face.

"Thank you as well, Estella," Ember replied to her friend. "Could you tell me what everyone is talking about?"

"More or less, they're talking about her. A white-haired girl being led around the school by... well, you. Some think that you may be bullying her, which is one of the reasons your aunt came to see you."

"S-she's not bullying me," Snow said, upset that people would jump to conclusions without getting the facts first.

"I know that, but there's nothing that can be done to stop them. If you want, I can stay with you and help dispel some rumors. Plus, this could allow me to show you some more magic."

Snow blushed again, finishing off her drink and chocolate bar to try to calm herself down.

"So, what would you like to do?

Chapter 8

"If there are going to be rumors about Snow because she is with me, then I can't hide this any longer," Ember said, determined to tell Snow everything. "Though I think it would be best to go somewhere more private to discuss this."

Many other students were already starting to gather around to get a look at Snow, and Ember wasn't comfortable talking about her past in front of others.

"If that's the case, let's go," Estella said, holding her hands out for the two girls. "If you're going to talk, then I'll be there for support."

"Thank you, Estella," Ember said, taking her hand, as did Snow. "There should be an empty classroom where we can discuss this."

Once inside the classroom, Estella locked the door and sat down beside Snow, holding her hands because she knew this story too well.

"There is no proper way for me to start this, so it might be easier to explain everything so that you can understand," Ember said, trying to figure out where she should begin. "To begin with, I have a sister. She is a kind, nerdy, and energetic girl, or at least she was."

"I won't sugarcoat it; I hated her—no, it's more accurate to say I resented her. Tanya adopted both of us when we were five. She treated us like we were her daughters and gave us everything we could ever want. Still, it was clear to me whom she loved more."

"My sister excelled at everything she did. Whether it was math, science, or history, she was always the best. At first, I tried to keep up with her and even attempted to surpass her, but I never succeeded. Over time, my resentment toward her continued to grow."

"All I ever wanted was to prove myself, but I allowed my desire to excel to become a grudge. I don't know when it happened, but at one point, I just gave up."

"For a while, it was nice not to care about what others thought and not to stress over achieving something I knew I could never accomplish. But that only lasted a short time, as my anger always surfaced again whenever I saw our mother giving the affection meant for both of us solely to her."

"I hated it so much. Why wouldn't she look at me the same way she looked at my sister? Why? Was I not good enough for her? Did I have to live my life in my sister's shadow just to be acknowledged by my mother?"

"These questions haunted my mind and only increased my anger, but I couldn't show my frustration toward her. Instead, I started to bully other students. I made their lives miserable, tormenting them because I could. They couldn't stop me because the principal was my mother. That was also why they never tried to report me. At the time, I enjoyed it; I took pleasure in watching others suffer."

"Though karma had a twisted way of getting back at me. On a rainy day six months ago, my sister finally confronted me about my bullying of the other students on the way home from school. Not only was she disappointed in me, but she also felt sorry for me. Yes, she felt sorry for me. I was a cruel person who took pleasure in tormenting others, yet she dared to feel compassion for me!"

Tears began to flow from Ember's eyes as her emotions intensified.

"I couldn't take it anymore, and I exploded on her. Everything I had been holding back for years spilled out of my mouth. At that moment, I felt incredible, but what happened next I couldn't undo. While I was distracted, reveling in the fact that I finally said what I had always wanted to say to her, I didn't realize I had stepped onto the road. Nor did I notice the oncoming car..."

"Before I knew what had happened, I found myself on the ground with scraped knees and the sound of people screaming behind me. At the time, I wanted to convince myself that what occurred was nothing more than a bad dream, but it wasn't. When I turned around, I saw her unconscious body on the ground."

"When the ambulance arrived, she was rushed to the hospital, but I wasn't allowed to go with her. By the time my mom arrived to pick me up, I couldn't say anything. All I could do was think about how this was all my fault. None of this would be happening if it weren't for me."

"We waited eight hours in the E.R., as the doctors did everything in their power to save her life. In the end, she was saved, but she ended up in a coma. The doctor said that even if she wakes up, she will never be able to walk again."

"For the first week, I never left her side, hoping she would wake up. I wanted to apologize to her for everything I had ever done. Soon after, my bullying of other students was revealed, and I was given three months of suspension. It would have been better if I had been expelled."

It was during this time that rumors started spreading that I was the one who pushed her into the car in an attempt to kill her. I became a pariah, as the bully turned into the bullied.

"I did nothing to stop them. They had every right to hate me. I spent the first month living like that, if you could even call it living. I barely ate, and most of my time was spent going to my suspension classes and going to the hospital."

"It wasn't long after the accident that her friends came down to visit her every few days. It's an understatement to say they hated me, and I couldn't blame them. I would stay to the side whenever they were there, knowing she would want to be closer to them than to me."

"This continued until one day when Faye opened up to me, yelling everything she hated about me before falling into my arms. I didn't understand why she would do such a thing, but she did. Eventually, the others started to open up to me as well. They helped me through a dark time, and so did Estella. Estella wasn't one of my sister's friends, but my own before I started bullying. Each of them supported me when I was at my lowest."

"After that, I soon started going to counseling with my mom. It's something we both needed after all that had happened. It brought us closer together. I want my sister to wake up more than anything in the world. I want to apologize to her. I want to get on my hands and knees, telling her that she doesn't have to forgive me because I was, no, I am a terrible person."

"That's the truth of the rumors," Ember said, wiping her tears away, knowing that Snow would now look at her with the same scorn as everyone else.

Snow's hand touched Ember's cheek, wiping away her remaining tears.

Snow couldn't believe what she had heard. Ember had been through too much. She understood why the other students hated her, but that was something she could never do. She could never hate her for her mistakes since the person she is now has learned from them and become a better person.

"It's a-alright," Snow said, allowing Ember to know that she wouldn't hate her for this. "I don't blame you.

Ember couldn't stop herself from hugging Snow and crying into her chest. "I'm sorry. I'm a terrible person!"

"You're not," Snow said, hugging her tighter. "Terrible people don't regret what they've done. Your sister won't blame you. If she did, she wouldn't have saved you. She loves you."

"She's right," Estella said, placing her hand on Ember's shoulder. For so long, Ember had been holding back her tears. She needed this. She needed someone who wouldn't judge her based on prejudice. The other girls were great, but it took them time to understand that Ember had changed. Snow didn't need that time and only viewed Ember as the person she was now.

"T-thank you," Ember said a few minutes later, wiping her tears from her face. She didn't expect to start crying like that, so she felt a bit embarrassed. "I'm glad that you believe me. It's hard trying to make up for my past mistakes, but it makes it easier when there are people who believe in me."

"Ember, that's what I've been telling you this entire time," Estella said, smiling at her friend.

"I'm sorry. I know I should listen to you more often. I should have…"

Ember blushed when she heard their stomachs growl. "Sorry, I think that I'm a bit hungry right now. Would you both like to head down to the cooking club with me next?"

"Ember, are you sure?" Estella asked her, aware of the kind of person who was there right now. There was a reason only two members in the cooking club, and that girl was the reason.

"The cooking club is your club, right?" Snow asked, curious to see.

"It is," Ember said, understanding why Estella looked nervous, but she still wanted to go regardless. After crying, she always found it best to indulge in some ice cream. Luckily, she had a small stash hidden in the back.

"Do you want to come with me? She should still be baking right now, and we might get lucky and get something fresh to eat."

"Lucky?" Estella said, rubbing her stomach, remembering the last time she went to the cooking club with Ember. She felt nauseous every time she thought about returning to that club.

"I think I'll pass on that, but in exchange, you should both stop at the auditorium afterward. I'll have a special show prepared for both of you."

"A m-magic show?" Snow asked, recalling the rose Estella pulled out from behind her ear earlier.

"Why, of course! As a powerful magician, I will prepare a special magic show just for the two of you. To make that happen, I must not waste any more time!"

Estella hurried out of the room, eager to make her next move unforgettable for Snow. She planned to perform such an impressive magic trick that Snow would beg to be her helper. A charming girl like her was perfect for the role.

"So, I guess we get some food and then a magic show," Ember said, rising to her feet and holding out her hand for Snow to take.

Snow took Ember's hand, which led her to the cooking club.

Once there, she nervously stood by the door, hearing loud noises coming from within.

"Um, Ember, is this the right place?" Snow asked, worried about what was happening in the room before her.

"It most certainly is, come on!"

Without waiting for a response, Ember walked into the room, allowing Snow to follow after her. Once inside, Snow was surprised to see only one girl with poofy, frizzy brown-and-gold hair, wearing a white shirt and a black skirt with an apron, running around the kitchen.

"Hmm, these need two more minutes, these need five, and wait, this… ah, one minute to go! Now to add the chocolate to this and the marshmallows to this one!"

Snow couldn't believe what she was seeing. This poofy, frizzy-haired girl was cooking, or rather, baking ten different things at once. How was this possible?

"Hmm, Ember, good thing you're here," the girl said, noticing Ember but failing to see Snow. "Stove eight is almost done, and then the cake in stove three needs to be flipped."

"Got it," Ember replied, putting on a pink apron before getting to work.

Uncertain of what to do, Snow sat quietly, watching the two girls as they finished baking. It was thrilling to see the table filled with baked goods: cookies, cakes, brownies, and much more. It was amazing.

"Perfect!" the poofy, frizzy-haired girl exclaimed, untying her apron. "I thought I would never get done. Now it's time to… huh? Who are you? Were you drawn in by the delicious smell of my food?" She was curious to see the frail, white-haired girl staring at her in awe.

"Oh shoot, I got caught up in the moment," Ember said, resisting the urge to eat the delicious food before her. "This is Snow. She's the girl that I told you all about."

"So you're the girl that won over her dense heart," the girl said to Snow, extending her hand, which Snow curiously took.

"The name's Diana, nice to meet you!"

Chapter 9

"I'm S-Snow," she said, shaking Diana's hand. "Your food smells so good."

It was hard not to compliment this girl. The scent of all the food she cooked filled the room, making her want to try some.

"Diana is the best baker around," Ember said proudly. "She's taught me everything I know.

"You both are making me blush, but there's no time for that. For now, it's time that we eat!"

"Eat?" Snow didn't know if it was fair for her to eat the food that Diana made. She wasn't the one who made it, nor did she help.

"Of course! I didn't make this food so that it couldn't be eaten. And by the looks of it, you could use a big meal. It looks like you're the same size as Rae. In my opinion, that girl does not eat enough. She needs to eat, and you do, too. Here, try this." Diana cut out a piece of chocolate cake and gave it to Snow.

"Are you sure?" Snow asked, concerned that she was being a bother.

"Of course, I'm sure," Diana said, handing her a fork. "And if you like, I can teach you a few cooking tricks myself later."

"Go on. I promise that you will like it," Ember said, already eating a slice of cake of her own.

"Alright…"

Snow slowly took a bite from the cake, and it was amazing. Never before had she tasted a cake that melted in her mouth. The proportions were perfect, and the taste was unimaginable. Before Snow could realize it, she had eaten the entire slice of cake that was given to her.

"My, my, my, it looks like one slice of cake wasn't enough," Diana said, glad to see that this small and frail-looking girl had an appetite. "Here, try a slice of blueberry pie next."

"But I j-just ate the cake?"

Snow tried to wipe any chocolate that got on her face while she was eating. There was no way she could eat any more than this. It would upset her stomach. Unfortunately for her, she did not realize Diana's true nature.

Diana loved to bake more than anything else, and she also loved watching people enjoy her food. She was happy that Ember had joined her club, as she was a glutton who never gained or lost weight, possessing a body that all girls dreamed of. Diana was a bit on the chubby side, but she didn't care much, as she knew she was perfect the way she was.

Diana was overjoyed to see that Snow was here. She could finally have a new person to taste her food. The other girls didn't like eating as much as she and Ember did. When Ember invited Estella over, she tried to fill Estella up with tons of food, but in the end, she ran out of the room only after eating five slices of cake.

"It's okay," Diana said to Snow. "Go on… eat."

"Alright."

Snow was unable to say no to her. She didn't want to hurt her feelings by refusing her generosity.

"…"

"And how about this one?" Diana said, placing even more food before Snow when she finished.

"Or what about this one? Or this one? Try this one. You'll love this. And this, oh, and don't forget this. And what about… hmm, are you alright?"

"I'm…ugh… fine," Snow said, feeling sick after eating so much food.

"Hmm? Oh no! Not again!" Ember, who had eaten as much as Snow, had finally realized that Diana was up to her old antics of forcing people to eat. "Snow, are you alright?"

"I'm…ugh…okay," Snow said, wanting nothing more than to lie down and fall asleep. She felt she had eaten enough to be full for the rest of the week.

"Diana, we talked about this."

Ember placed her hand over Snow's forehead to discover she had a fever. She must have pushed herself too far today. She needed rest.

"I'm sorry."

Diana realized what she had done. She knew she should have been more considerate of Snow and shouldn't have forced her to eat so much, but she couldn't help herself.

"Here, this should help," Diana said, pulling out a tonic to help ease Snow's stomach pains.

"Thank you," Snow said, drinking the tonic. "Your food is g-good. I want to try it again sometime."

"Well, if you insist."

"I think… I think that I… I sleep." Snow couldn't resist the pull of sleep for much longer and closed her eyes, falling asleep.

"Diana, help me bring her to the nurse's office. I'll call her guardian to pick her up," Ember said, smiling at the girl who fell asleep in her arms.

Chapter 10

"Ngh... m-mom, don't leave me," Snow muttered as she dreamt of the day she was abandoned at the orphanage. She hadn't had this dream in a while. Why now?

"It's all right, sweetie, I'm here," a gentle voice said, soothing her as a warm hand tenderly caressed her cheeks.

When Snow opened her eyes, she was surprised to see Autumn sitting beside her. Why was she here? Wait, where was she?

"How are you feeling?" Autumn asked, smiling as Snow called her mom. While she may have been dreaming when she said it, Autumn still decided to count it.

"Where am I?" Snow asked, concerned, wondering if she was in the hospital again.

"You're in the school nurse's office. It seems that you passed out after overeating. You have a slight fever, but the nurse says it's due to overstimulation from a new environment."

"When I got the call from the nurse telling me that you had collapsed, I rushed over here as fast as I could. I'm glad that it's nothing too serious."

Autumn was happy that Snow was all right and that she could have some fun today. However, she hoped that when Snow started attending classes, she'd take things easy.

"Snow, are you alright?" Ember asked, popping her head out from behind Autumn. She was so worried when Snow collapsed that she couldn't leave her side.

"I'm… I'm all right," Snow said to them, happy that people in her life cared about her like this. "Though I think I'm full."

Her stomach still hurt a bit from all the food that Diana had made her eat, but she was feeling better than before.

"Then I guess I'll make a nice, easy-to-swallow soup for you tonight," Autumn said, unable to hold back a laugh.

"Alright."

"Good. Now, I'm going to talk to the nurse to make sure it's alright to take you home. Ember, please stay with her."

"Are you feeling better?" Ember asked Snow, still worried. "I'm sorry, I should have warned you about Diana's tendencies. She didn't mean any harm by it. She loves watching people eat her food."

"It's f-fine. It was good." Snow couldn't hate Diana for feeding her so much. Despite being half forced to eat, she couldn't help but think it was delicious. "Though I think less will be better next time."

"Yeah, it will. Oh yeah, Diana did give me these for you," Ember said, pulling out a small bottle of pills.

"These should help with digesting all the food you just ate. She said taking one of these a day for a week should be more than enough."

"Thanks. "

Snow didn't know what else to say. She never thought she would meet so many amazing people today.

"Alright, sweetie, the nurse says you should be good to leave anytime now," Autumn said, returning from her talk with the nurse.

She discussed how this could be a safe haven for Snow while she attended school. If she felt any discomfort, physical or mental, she was always welcome here, no matter the time of day.

"Are you ready to go home now?"

"But I haven't seen everything yet."

Snow was disappointed. She wanted to see more of the school and meet more of Ember's friends.

"Sweetie, you need to rest. You can come back tomorrow."

Autumn saw how eager Snow was to explore more, and it hurt her that she couldn't let Snow continue her tour, but her health came first. Being a parent meant doing what was best for their children, even if it meant not giving them what they wanted.

"Um, excuse me, ma'am, if I may, I have a suggestion." Ember knew that Autumn was right and that it was probably best for Snow to go home and rest, but she had an idea that could help.

"Snow and I were invited to a private magic show by a friend of mine. She's been preparing things for a while now, and it would be a shame if she couldn't do it."

"Please~." Snow really wanted to go. She liked Estella and was interested in seeing a magic show for the first time. "Can we please watch the show?

"Ember, do you promise this show won't stress her out?" Autumn asked, making sure things would be safe for Snow before agreeing.

"I promise. The only thing that Snow will feel is excitement. Estella is a pretty good, after all. You'll be amazed by what she can do. It's almost like real magic."

"Fine, but nothing stressful, alright?"

"Don't worry. I texted her to tell her to keep any stressful elements out of the show."

Ember showed her text to Estella, demonstrating to Autumn that she didn't intend to make another mistake.

"Alright, you can go, but I'm coming with you." Autumn wasn't going to let Snow out of her sight, fearful that she might pass out again. "And before we go, you need to drink something; it will help."

Autumn handed Snow an energy drink to help her stay hydrated and regain some of her energy.

"Thank y-you."

Snow drank the energy drink without question, knowing Autumn was looking out for her.

"Very good. Now let me help you up," Autumn said, assisting Snow to her feet.

Snow felt a bit woozy, but she was certain this would pass.

Ember led the way to the auditorium, where Estella prepared her show for them. When she opened the doors, it was finally time for the show to begin.

Chapter 11

"Welcome One And All To The Greatest Show Of All Time!!!" Estella yelled the moment the door opened.

"She really loves going over the top like this," Ember said, happy to see Estella enjoying herself.

"Hmm. What's this? It looks like we have a little chatterbug in the audience. How about we see them fly?"

"Fly? What is she-woah~!" All of a sudden, Ember began to rise into the air as if she were flying, with a dim spotlight highlighting her every move.

"Estella! What's going on?"

"Worry not, ladies. This little chatterbug has nothing to fear. Now, please, if you are all seated, we can continue with her punishment!"

"Amazing. How is she doing that?" Autumn asked as they watched Ember flail around. She was forced to fly in the air, moving in the direction Estella's wand pointed.

"It… it looks fun."

Snow couldn't help but wish to be the one up in the air flying, but she knew that she would be far too frightened if she were.

"Estella! Put me down!" Ember yelled, terrified, still unaware of the method Estella was using to hold her.

"My, my. It appears that this naughty little bug wants to be put out of its misery. To that request, I say sure, no problem," Estella said as two human-sized containers materialized behind her in a puff of smoke.

"In the left container is a horde of piranhas, and on my right is a container filled with whipped cream. I wonder which one I should place her in?"

"My dear audience, raise your left hand for piranhas and your right hand for the whipped cream."

Not wanting to see Ember harmed, both Autumn and Snow raised their right hands.

"Alright! It looks like the choice is obvious! It's punishment time!" Estella pointed her wand down towards the whipped cream, and seconds later, Ember fell right inside of it.

Snow couldn't help but let out a small laugh, hoping to see Ember covered in whipped cream from head to toe.

"Now let's see what this little chatterbug has to say now!"

"..."

"Ember, you can come out now," Estella said, sounding worried for Ember. "Come on, Ember, I know that you can't stay in there forever. ...Ember?"

Despite her calling Ember several times, there was no answer.

"Excuse me, folks, it seems our little chatterbug is hiding from us. I guess that leaves me with no choice but to drag her out myself," she said, climbing the stairs next to the container and peering down inside it.

"Hmm, that's odd, where did she go?" Estella asked curiously, looking down into the container of whipped cream. As she did, something amazing happened. Ember emerged from behind in a stunning white dress, slowly making her way up behind Estella.

Snow was baffled by what she was seeing, and I felt a bit embarrassed as she had a strange desire to be up there on stage with them.

"Hmm, I'm sorry, everyone, but it seems our chatterbug has vanished," Estella said without looking back. If she had, she would have seen Ember standing right behind her.

"Still calling me a bug now, aren't we?" Ember said to her. "I would rather you call me the Great and Powerful Ember!" Before Estella could react, she was pushed into the whipped cream, disappearing inside it.

"My, my, my. It looks like a new lead magician is needed to continue this show! Now, how about we get a—"

"Stop right there, imposter!" another Ember yelled, storming her way from the back just as the first Ember had, wearing the same dress.

This was blowing Snow's mind. How was this possible? There was no way that there could be two Embers. What was going on here?

"Imposter? You're the imposter!" the original Ember yelled at her. "It's obvious that you're Estella, trying to take back the show! Sorry, dear, but your time is up, and it is time for someone else to take on the role of lead performer!"

"How dare you! I'm the real Ember!" the second one said, but based on what the first Ember noted, there was no way the second one was Ember. It had to be Estella.

"Hmm, now this is quite the issue we have here," the original Ember said. "How about a little help from a member of the audience?"

"Surprisingly, I agree with this impostor," the second Ember replied. "How about you, the girl with white hair? Please come on up and help us figure out the truth."

"Oh, this is so exciting! Who is the real one?" Autumn wondered, trying to decipher the trick. "Go on, Snow, have some fun," she urged her.

"That's right! Right this way!" both Embers called to her, holding out their hands. Upon taking their hands, both Embers pulled her up onto the stage.

"Now then, our lovely member of the audience, which one of us is the real Ember?" the original Ember asked, speaking strangely.

"Um, is it her?" Snow asked, pointing to the second Ember.

"What? No way! It's her!" the original Ember yelled in shock. "She's the impostor!"

"Oh really?" the second Ember said, walking over and ripping off the mask covering the original Ember's face, revealing her to be none other than Estella!

"No! Fair! How did you know?" Estella yelled, curious as to how Snow knew the truth.

"Because it just seemed too obvious?" Snow said, wondering how the trick was done.

"Hmm, it would seem that I did overdo it a bit," Estella said back to her. "Despite that, I believe our audience member deserves a reward. My lovely assistant, if you would."

"Why, most certainly, my dear imposter," Ember said, teasing Estella for being found out after all her work to pull off this trick.

They began to spin around Snow, encasing her body in their dresses.

Snow started to get dizzy as they spun around her, unaware that by the time they stopped, her clothes had been replaced with the exact same dress that they were wearing.

"OMG! So cute!" Autumn yelled from her seat, snapping as many pictures as she could with her phone.

"My, my, my. Our new assistant looks wonderful, now doesn't she?" Estella said, showing Snow her new look, pulling a mirror out of nowhere.

"Is… is this me?" Snow asked in awe of the dress she was wearing.

"Oh, of course it is, silly, and with this dress, you are officially The Great And Powerful Estella's newest assistant!"

"What?" No way. I c-can't stand up on stage," Snow said nervously.

"But you're already here, so why not have some fun?" Ember said to her, noticing that Snow wasn't entirely opposed to this idea.

"I guess…"

Snow didn't want to disappoint them since they went out of their way to do this for her. There was no way that she could say no.

"Perfect! Now come this way as we make your body disappear!" Estella yelled, making Snow feel just as nervous as she was led toward a giant human-sized cross casket. "Step right on in."

"Go on, it's all right," Ember reassured her.

Trusting Ember, Snow stepped into the cross, allowing Estella to close it and cover her entire body, especially her head. Oddly enough, Snow could feel something strange and squishy touching her. Though she looked through the cracks, she couldn't see anything.

"Ladies and well, just ladies, allow me to show you a disappearing act like no other! What say you, my dear assistant, should we start with the legs or arms?"

"Legs?" Snow didn't understand what she meant. How was this supposed to be a disappearing act?

'You heard her. It's time for the legs to go!" Estella yelled as Ember removed the part of the cross that covered her legs, revealing that it was made up of sections.

"What? How is that possible?" Autumn yelled from her seat as she saw that the moment Ember removed that part of the cross, Snow's legs were no longer there.

"My legs!" Snow yelled nervously. She could still feel her legs, but she couldn't see them. What was happening? How was Estella doing this?

"Don't worry, my lovely assistant. I promise you will return to normal once the show ends. Ember and I wouldn't lie to you," Estella said to her, reassuring Snow that she was safe right now. There was nothing for her to fear.

"Now, let's go for her arms next!" Estella instructed Ember to take off the arms of the cross, revealing Snow's arms to be gone as well. Just as with her legs, Snow could feel her hands, but she couldn't see them. Her arms felt heavy, and she could not move them much, but she could tell that there was something on her arms.

"Alright, now for the chest!" Estella happily said, helping Ember remove the last piece, making it look like Snow's head was floating in the air.

"Amazing! Snow, you're doing great!" Autumn yelled, extremely impressed by the show.

"And now to bring her back!" Estella yelled as she and Ember began to piece Snow back together, placing the pieces of the cross back on her before taking it off as a whole. "And… oh my, I don't think this was supposed to happen."

Snow looked down and saw that her entire body was mangled! Her right arm was where her left leg should be. Her left foot was where her right hand was supposed to be. And everything was a mess! She was so scared that she couldn't move.

"Now, don't worry, everyone; I can fix this." Estella didn't look nervous at all. She looked excited as Ember brought over a large black tarp. Without waiting, they threw the tarp over Snow, covering her in darkness. When they did, Snow could feel whatever was on her body slowly slip off, and before she knew it, they were ripping the tarp off.

"Tada! Restored to her perfect beauty! Thank you, one and all, for joining us today! Sadly, this is all I could prepare with the time I had."

"Bravo! Bravo!" Autumn yelled, running up on stage to make sure that Snow wasn't too scared by what happened with the last trick.

"You did wonderfully. If you'd like, we should do this again sometime," Estella said, happy to have such a cute assistant to work with.

"You should! You did great!" Ember congratulated Snow for being brave despite being dragged into the show.

"Thanks… the show was a-amazing."

Snow couldn't help but be impressed by everything that happened. While the last trick did scare her, she trusted Ember and knew that no harm would come to her. She was glad that she got to take an active role. Perhaps she might try this again in the future, but only with friends. There was no way that she could manage doing this in front of a crowd.

"I knew she would like it," Estella said triumphantly. "If I had more time to prepare, I could have shown you my cannon teleporting trick. However, I guess I can save that for next time."

"You truly were amazing. Who would have thought that a high school student, could prepare such complex tricks." Autumn was glad that she had come to this. This wasn't even Snow's first day, and she had already made such an interesting friend.

"Thanks. I learned a lot from my dad. He's usually on tour, but it's always fun to test new magic tricks out with him when he's home."

"I'm sure he would be very proud of you. You know, since you gave us quite an amazing show, I think we owe you a small favor. How about we treat you to dinner sometime after Snow gets settled with her classes?" Autumn said to Estella.

"I would love that! It's a date!"

Chapter 12

As the weeks went by, Autumn fulfilled her promise by picking up Snow, Ember, and Estella after school.

During these few weeks, Snow had grown attached to Estella just as she had with Ember. Thanks to them, Snow's school days were full of fun.

Alright, girls. Since Snow is finally getting her bearings here, I think we should get something to eat. My treat!

"You don't have to. We can pay for ourselves," Estella said. While glad she was invited, she wasn't someone who took money from others.

"Nonsense. Thanks to you girls, Snow is enjoying her school life. Just look, she doesn't seem to mind," Autumn pulled Snow over to her and showed her Snow's nervous expression.

"Y-you should come, s-since we're friends," Snow said, using all her courage to call them her friends.

"Of course, we'll go," Ember and Estella said simultaneously. Neither of them wanted to make Snow sad by saying no.

"Great! It's decided!" Autumn said happily, clapping her hands together before driving them down to a lovely family diner that was not far from here.

"Alright, girls, don't be afraid to order whatever you like. Though I do hope you won't try to break my wallet that much," she said as they were given their menus. She couldn't help but feel happy knowing that Snow had made such good friends.

"Um… can I try this? Snow is nervous at first, looking at the menu to see a cute parfait.

"Snow, you've eaten way too many sweets. Eating something healthy to clean out your stomach would be best."

"Okay."

Snow felt a little disappointed, but she knew Autumn was just looking out for her, even though she really had quite the sweet tooth.

"Here, I recommend this," Ember said, unable to hold back her laughter. "It should be healthy enough and leave extra room for that parfait."

"Thank you," Snow said to her before they all ordered their food.

"Oh my, Estella, are you sure you don't want to eat more than that?" Autumn asked, noticing that Estella had only ordered a salad.

"I'm fine. My mom has a big meal waiting for me at home."

Estella smiled wearily at them, worrying Snow.

"Oh my, I'm sorry! I should have asked if either of you had plans before taking you. I'm terribly sorry," Autumn said, concerned that her eagerness to talk with Snow's friends had inconvenienced them.

"No, no, no, it's fine," Estella said. "Going out to eat is nice, and I couldn't refuse such a kind offer."

"Alright, but please tell me next time if you have plans to eat. I wouldn't want your mother's hard work to go to waste."

"Yeah… hard work."

"Hmm? What was that, sweetie?" Autumn asked, slightly noticing the sadness in Estella's voice, though she couldn't quite hear what she said.

I was saying that my mother is a very hardworking woman, though sometimes I wish she could be more like... well, like you.

"Oh my, you're ever so kind, but you shouldn't wish for anyone else to be your mother than the one you have right now.

Snow and the others had a great time while they ate. Both she and Estella remained quiet for most of the meal, while Ember and Autumn got along quite well. Snow was worried about Estella but didn't know the right words to express her concern.

Her concern persisted from the moment they left the dinner to dropping off Ember, and even while dropping off Estella. Even though they hadn't known each other for long, she could definitely tell that something was wrong.

"Thank you once again for the nice meal and ride back," Estella said to Autumn as she stepped out of the car. "And I hope to see you in school soon, Snow."

"Same," Snow replied, taking a bite of the parfait she got to go from dinner.

"Don't mention it, sweetie. I do hope that we can do it again sometime, perhaps with your mother,"

Autumn said, noticing a shadow in the lit window of Estella's home.

"Yeah, sure. I have to go," Estella said as she returned to her home.

"What a nice girl. You truly picked out a wonderful friend… Snow? Snow, are you listening?"

"Y-yes," Snow replied, disturbed by what she just saw through the window of Estella's home. She couldn't tell for sure, but she could have sworn that Estella's mother just hit her.

"Snow? Sweetie, your parfait is melting. Are you feeling alright?"

"I'm not hungry anymore," Snow said, looking down at the melting parfait.

"Alright, sweetie. We can put it in the fridge when we get home."

"Okay…"

"Sweetie, is there something bothering you?"

"Do you hit Lily?" Snow asked, unsure if what she saw was normal.

"What? Snow, I would never harm Lily," Autumn said, shocked by what Snow had asked her. "While she may be rude at times, hitting her is never something I could ever do. She is my precious daughter, just as you are. I could never hit either of you. Where did this question come from?"

"Estella's m-mom hit her."

Snow had never had a mother or someone like Autumn to take care of her before. When she saw Estella's mother hit her, she was uncertain if something like that was natural.

"She what?" Autumn turned off the car's engine, furious at what she had just heard. "Snow, are you saying that you saw Estella's mother lay a finger on her?"

"Y-yes."

Snow felt a bit scared. The expression on Autumn's face was filled with malice. She never thought that such a kind woman could look like this.

"Alright then, sweetie, I think we should say hi to her before we leave," Autumn said, presenting herself with a smile that sent shivers down Snow's spine.

Autumn led Snow out of the car toward Estella's and rang the doorbell. When the door opened, Snow and Autumn were shocked by what they saw.

In front of them, gripping the door frame, was an older woman with messy pale blonde hair. She wasn't wearing any pants, exposing her more than vulgar self, and a loose top that looked like it might slip off. In her hands was a bottle of wine.

"Who the hell are you?" the woman asked, not even bothering to be concerned with how she looked.

"Excuse me, ma'am, I am Autumn Dust, and this is Snow; we were the ones who just dropped off Estella, but it seems she left something in our car. You wouldn't mind if we gave it back to her?"

"Just drop it on the ground; that little brat can pick it up in the morning," the woman said, to Autumn's surprise.

"Excuse me?"

Autumn could tell that this was Estella's mother based on her appearance alone, but after hearing what she had just said, she had to ignore that thought. No true mother would ever call their child a brat.

"Did I stutter?" the woman said, teetering back and forth, trying to lift the bottle. "Throw whatever the heck you have of hers on the ground and get off my property!"

"Ma'am, there is no need to yell," Autumn said, trying to calm herself. "Just allow us to hand what we have over to Estella, and then we can go."

"I said get out!" The woman quickly resorted to violence, lifting the bottle of wine and pouring much of its contents onto herself before trying to strike Autumn with it.

"STOP!" Estella grabbed her mother's arms, stopping her from hitting Autumn.

"E-Estel…" Snow couldn't say a word when she saw the giant bruise across Estella's face. Was that from what she just saw?

"You brat! Let go of me!" the woman said, struggling to break free from Estella, only to fall to the ground herself.

"I'm sorry, but my mom is a bit drunk," Estella said with a weak smile. "She didn't mean to be rude. I'm sure that if you met her on any other day, things would be different."

"You stupid brat! Let go of me!" she yelled again as Estella gently pulled the bottle out of her hands. "I should never have had you!"

"Hah… she doesn't mean that," Estella said with a worried laugh, unable to meet their gaze.

"Sweetie, your eye."

Autumn couldn't believe the condition Estella's mother was in. How could she behave like this in front of her child?

"It's nothing," Estella said, ashamed that they noticed it.

"Estella?" Snow was worried about her. She was clearly hurt, but why wasn't she admitting it?

"Sweetie, please, if you need help, just tell us," Autumn said, knowing that she couldn't do anything unless the girl told her she needed help.

There were always many cases of children being abused by their parents, but sadly, nothing can be done. Unless the child says they need help, there's little she can do.

"You should go," Estella said to them, unable to let them see her like this.

"But sweetie—"

"I said, just go." Estella didn't want them to see her cry. She had to endure this. It was the only choice she had.

"Alright," Autumn said to her, realizing why Estella refused to admit that she needed help after a glance at the interior of her home. "Snow, we should go."

"But Estella." Snow didn't want to leave her alone with the woman. She didn't want to see her get hurt.

"This isn't something you should concern yourself with," she said, brushing Snow's worries aside. "Just go home."

"Y-yeah! Get the fuck out of here!" the woman yelled as Autumn led Snow back to the car. However,

Snow didn't sit in front with Autumn this time; she sat in the back seat, refusing to even look at Autumn. How could she turn her back on Estella? It wasn't fair.

"I'm sorry, sweetie," Autumn couldn't bear to leave that poor girl behind. Her precious daughter was crying in the back seat because of that woman. She would not let things end here. That woman was going to get exactly what she deserved.

Chapter 13

Autumn wasted no time contacting Tanya after Snow fell asleep. She didn't even bother to look at her before heading to her room. Autumn felt heartbroken that she had made Snow feel this way. She needed to do whatever it took to regain her trust.

"Autumn? Why are you calling at this hour?" Tanya asked at the end of the phone. She had told her to call whenever she needed help with Snow, but it was quite late into the night.

"I need your help to save one of your students. After seeing what happened tonight, there's no way I can let this slide."

Autumn proceeded to tell Tanya everything that had happened while thinking of a plan to help Estella. She couldn't allow this poor girl to suffer any longer.

"I never knew," Tanya said, shocked to hear that one of her students was in such a predicament right now. "Estella is always a bright and energetic student. I never would have thought that she was living this way. I will set up a meeting with her mother and the guidance counselor. I'll do everything in my power to help."

"Alright, thank you for your help," Autumn said, knowing there was only so much that she could do without evidence. Hopefully, they could save this poor girl.

The weekend flew by, yet Snow still refused to talk to Autumn, convinced she had abandoned Estella. Even when Autumn accompanied her to school, Snow remained silent.

"Have a good day at school," Autumn said, waving her off before meeting with Tanya. However, Snow didn't even bother to glance back at her. She believed she could resolve this misunderstanding with Tanya's help.

Snow had no desire to engage with Autumn. She felt responsible for Estella's hurt and had done nothing to help. She thought Autumn was different, but it seemed she was mistaken. As she entered her first class, Snow couldn't stop thinking about Estella. She needed to find her.

However, despite wanting to meet with her, she couldn't. She wasn't in their shared class, nor was she in the halls or cafeteria. Before she knew it, the day had ended in a flash, and Estella was nowhere to be seen.

She would have to look for her again tomorrow since it was time for her to go to the principal's office and inform her how her first few weeks had been. She had expected that it would just be a normal meeting, but when she got to the office, no one else was around, though she could hear voices coming through the crack in the door.

Not knowing what to do, Snow carefully peered through the crack of the door to see Principal Tanya and Autumn talking to... Estella's mom?

"I can't believe you called me out here over some baseless rumors," Estella's mom said. "This is nothing more than a waste of my time."

"False rumors? I was there!" Autumn yelled back at her, unable to refrain from shouting at this woman. "I saw her face!"

"Calm down, Autumn. There's no need to yell," Tanya said, ensuring the meeting was conducted as proper adults should. "Mrs. Moon, I need to know if what Autumn says is true. Did you lay a hand on your child?"

"Really? Did you make me cancel my spa session just to ask me such a stupid question?" she replied, clearly displeased about being there.

Unlike the night she met Estella, Estella's mom was now dressed in designer clothes and jewelry. It must have cost her a fortune. Snow couldn't believe she had the audacity to dress like that at school.

"I could give a rat's ass about what that girl does. I don't care for her enough to even look at her."

"Mrs. Moon, mind your language, please," Tanya told her. "Child abuse claims are serious. Handling this matter through the school is more beneficial for both parties than involving Child Services. If we can resolve this issue by figuring out what happened, wouldn't that be easier for you and your daughter?"

"Ugh, how annoying. I did not hit Estella. Are you happy?"

"Happy? This isn't about me being happy. This is about her safety," Autumn said to her. "I saw you that night so drunk that you couldn't even stand, and Estella with a black eye. How do you explain that she got that?"

"I don't know; maybe you were the one who gave it to her," Estella's mom said, trying to shift the blame. "Both you and your daughter were the last to see her before she came home. Then, to add insult to injury, you both returned to view your handiwork."

"What are you talking about?" Autumn was baffled. How could this woman openly lie about this with a smile spread across her face?

"I'm talking about how you and your so-called daughter assaulted my daughter. Perhaps I should now call the authorities and see what they say about this."

Was this woman serious? Snow couldn't believe what she was hearing. How could she claim that they were the ones who harmed Estella?

"Mrs. Moon, I would ask that you refrain from making such threats," Tanya said, baffled by this woman's gall. She had never met anyone this shameless before.

"And why should I? You think you have the right to tell me how to raise my kid. Your kid almost killed her sister, leaving her disabled. While your kid caused nothing but trouble at her private school, not to mention that little freak you just brought in. The same one you brought to my house. That ugly little brat only decided to get close to Estella because of her father."

"Let me guess that's the reason. Your daughter assaulted mine because she was a greedy little freak."

"You!"

"Autumn, stop!" Tanya grabbed Autumn before she could slap Estella's moon across the face. "There will be consequences if you harm her."

"Oh my, look at you, ready to hit me at a moment's notice," she said, arrogantly looking down at Autumn and Tanya. "You both can't do anything to me. So before you question my relationship with my daughter, you should take the time to take care of yours."

"Mrs. Moon, your words are uncalled for," Tanya said, trying to resist the urge to punch this woman in the face for what she said about her daughters, but she would lose her job as the principal if she did. She needed to be there to protect her daughter. "You owe us both an apology.

"I owe the two of you nothing. Not only do you waste my time, but you also accuse me of something you have no proof of. I don't care about what you saw on Estella's face because you never saw how she got it. More importantly, Estella will never tell you how she got it. So next time that either of you thinks about acting like a hero, don't. Stay out of my family affairs or else. I can have both of you put away for a long time."

She was a monster. Snow couldn't believe that someone like this was real. There was just no way that this woman thought she could get away with what she did to Estella.

"Fine, I can see that this conversation is a waste," Tanya said. "I shall inform Child Services to open up an investigation on this. I do hope that you will be prepared for what happens next."

"What the hell do I have to prepare for when it is the two of you that are going to lose your kids, not me!" Estella's mom yelled out arrogantly, storming out of the office and swinging the door open so hard that the corner hit Snow right in the head; she was knocked down to the ground, with Estella's mom standing over her.

Chapter 14

"Mom?" Estella yelled as she walked out of the vice principal's office, where she had been since her mother dragged her here today after refusing to let her attend classes. "What are you doing?"

"Ugh, because of you, I'm forced to be here, so be grateful, you little brat," Estella's mother retorted, indifferent to the fact that she insulted her daughter in public. "Now go back home; I'm sure you can find something useful to do there. It's much better than wasting your days practicing your ridiculous magic act."

"It's not ridiculous!" Snow yelled at her, slowly picking herself up. She wouldn't allow Estella's mom to insult her. She had to be brave for Estella.

"Hah? It's you, the one who assaulted my daughter," she said, attempting to paint Snow as the attacker from the other night.

"I d-didn't d-do anything… you attacked her," Snow stammered, feeling her legs start to shake from fear.

"You're so guilty that you can't even stop stuttering," Estella's mom mocked her.

"Stop! Leave her alone!" Estella yelled, stepping in front of Snow to protect her. As she did, Snow noticed a bruise mark peeking out from underneath her blouse sleeves.

"What's this? You can never stop embarrassing me in public now, can you? Here I am doing you a favor by standing up against the girl that hurt you, and now you're defending her?"

"I get called down here because you put it into people's minds that I'm abusing you. To think that I would raise a lying brat who would stand against her own mother. And to think after everything I have done for you, the both of you. Maybe I wasn't strict enough with you. Maybe you need to take a break from your magic tricks and illusions because they make you incapable of seeing the truth."

"Estella…"

Snow focused closer on the bruise and noticed patches of makeup covering her arms, realizing there was more happening than she understood.

"No! You wouldn't!" Estella yelled back at her mother. "You can't!"

"Can't I?" her mother replied smugly. "I'm the one who pays the bills, and it's my house that you live in. Who do you think you are to say that I can't decide if these silly magic tricks are done in my house or not?"

"Estella… are you…?"

Snow wanted to reach out to Estella, but she didn't get the chance.

"No! You can't stop me from doing what I love!" Estella yelled, furious that she had to endure this day after day. For so long, her mother had manipulated her, mocked her, and abused her. She didn't know exactly what triggered this outburst against her mother, but she needed to voice it.

"Really? Does that mean you're willing to abandon your obligations to your family and run off just like your father? That would leave just the two of us alone. Are you sure that you want that?" she asked, knowing that no matter what outburst Estella had, she would never defy her for long. She wouldn't let the girl who ruined her life run away.

"No... I..."

"Estella? Are you okay?" Snow asked, lightly running her fingers across one of the patches of makeup on Estella's arm, causing her to flinch in fear.

"Snow! What are you doing?" Estella yelled, scared, thinking that Snow saw her bruises. She had been rushed out today and had no time to cover them properly. She held the spot of her arm that Snow touched, doing her best to hide it from her.

"See! Look at this!" Estella's mother yelled, noticing that a small crowd was starting to form from all of their yelling. "This unruly girl attacked my daughter!" She roughly grabbed Estella's arm, wiping off the portion of makeup that Snow touched, showcasing the bruise for everyone to see.

"Is this how the daughter of the friend of your principal acts? Is she allowed to harm other students because she thinks she holds the power to do so? It's just like the girl who almost committed murder! This entire school is filled with problems!"

The other students started to gossip among themselves. None of them knew what was going on, but they could see a woman displaying her daughter's injury and claiming that the weak-looking, white-haired girl was the cause. She even brought up the matter with Ember.

"Are you happy now?" Estella's mother whispered into her ear. "Because of you, this girl will be a social outcast. "I hope you're happy."

"What is going on here?" Tanya yelled, storming out of her office with Autumn behind her, who wasted no time pulling Snow close. "This is not a show! Classes have already ended for the day; either proceed to your clubs or head home. This is a private matter."

Not wishing to get in trouble, the students did as they were told, leaving while they gossiped among themselves.

"What is all of this?" she asked furiously at Estella's mother.

"I was just showing your students what kind of monster this girl is," she said, arrogantly smiling at Snow, making her feel nauseous.

"Who gave you the right to belittle one of my students in front of her classmates? And who gave you the right to showcase your daughter's bruises? This is a school, not social media."

"So what? Do you expect me to sit still and do nothing?"

"I expect you to act like an adult," Tanya said to her, appalled by the audacity of this woman. "You owe both of these girls an apology."

"I owe them nothing."

Estella's mother didn't care because this was what she wanted. She wanted to make a scene so that she could be perceived as the victim. "Now get out of my way."

"Pathetic…"

Autumn had had enough of this woman, and now that they had more than enough proof, they could end her.

"What? What the hell did you say to me!" Estella's mother yelled at the top of her lungs, losing her cool for a split second.

"I said you're pathetic. Someone like you isn't fit to be a mother. Taking responsibility for one's actions is the cornerstone of being an adult. Those who refuse to see the error of their ways can only be seen as ignorant children."

"I don't have to answer you," Estella's mother said, trying to calm herself before grabbing Estella by the wrist and storming her out of the room. However, Autumn would not let her run away from this. She stood in the doorway to ensure she couldn't leave until she was done.

"Children are not objects that you can use to relieve your stress or make yourself out to be a victim. They are supposed to be loved and cared for to help them grow. If they do something wrong, you must punish them, but make sure they know you do not hate them and that you are there for them. It is your responsibility to help them grow into proper adults."

"I don't have to do anything," Estella's mother said back to Autumn. "What gives you the right to tell me how I should act and how I should raise my kid?"

"The right of a mother. As a mother, I can't stand by and let this happen to an innocent girl like this. I should have stood my ground when I first saw what happened. That was my failure and not one that I wish to make again. If I let this happen, what kind of example am I setting for my daughter?"

"…"

Snow couldn't react to what Autumn had said. Did she really see her as a daughter despite the way she had acted toward her these past few days? She didn't know how much Autumn actually cared for her or what she thought of her. She needed to give Autumn a proper apology when this was over.

"I don't care what kind of example you try to make for that freakish-looking girl. My daughter belongs to me, so don't you dare think you can tell me how to raise her." Estella's mother refused to listen, despite everything Autumn had said being true.

"That girl, no, Estella, doesn't belong to you. She doesn't belong to anyone," Autumn said, furious that Estella was being treated like an object after what she had just said.

"It's fine…"

Estella just wanted this to end. She knew it would only get worse the longer they fought against her mother. There was nothing to gain from this but pain.

"It's not fine!" Snow yelled, scared by the expression that Estella was making. "You're h-hurting!"

"Snow, it's not—agh!"

"Be quiet!" her mother yelled, yanking her arm and dragging her away, pushing Autumn aside. "All of you here will pay for trying to make a fool out of me. I will make sure of it!"

"Ma'am, you can't leave yet," Tanya said, worried about the poor girl.

"Shut up! I've had it with this school. I am suing you and removing her from school today!"

"What? No!"

Estella couldn't leave the school. If she couldn't go here, then there would be no point in living. Day after day, she suffered, and this was the only place where she could be herself. She didn't want to give it up.

"Quiet! I don't care what you have to say!" her mother yelled, yanking her arm harder, smearing even more of the makeup that hid her scars and bruises. "Get moving or… what the hell?"

"Squeak?"

Right in front of Estella's mom was a cute white bunny rabbit, one that looked oddly familiar to Snow, but she didn't know why.

"You freaks allow disgusting animals inside your school. This place is worse than I thought! Get away from me, you ugly thing!" Estella's mother yelled, attempting to kick the bunny, but then something amazing happened.

Out of nowhere, the bunny jumped into the air and kicked Estella's mother in the face.

"Argh!!! You vermin! How dare you! Ugh! My nose! It's bleeding!" she yelled furiously as she tried to cover her bleeding nose. "That's it. I have had it! Estella, bring yourself home today. I need to get this fixed! And don't you dare talk to them, or you know what will happen!" she yelled, storming out of the room, leaving everyone stunned by what just happened. But when they looked back, the bunny was gone.

Snow could have sworn that she saw a streak of pink walking by the edge of the window, but she didn't have time to worry about that.

"Estella!" Snow ran over to her friend, scared that she was hurt.

"Snow, please help her into my office," Tanya said, not wanting to make a bigger scene than it already was. This poor girl looked like she was about to cry.

"Estella…" Snow tried her best to lead Estella into Tanya's office, sitting her down so they could all talk.

"Estella, sweetie, please, it's clear what is going on," Autumn said. "I know that you may love your mother, but you can't live like this.

"… Don't …"

"What was that, sweetie?"

"I don't love her," Estella said, unable to hold back her tears.

Her mother had ruined everything. She didn't want anyone to get involved in her family problems, but now it was too late. No one would look at her the same way after this.

"Estella?" Snow held Estella's hands, trying to provide her with any form of relief. She wanted to do more for the girl who helped her smile, but she knew that this was all she could manage.

"Estella, is your mother abusing you?" Tanya asked gently, trying not to overwhelm the poor girl.

"No…" Estella couldn't tell them. It would be over if she spoke up, but she couldn't. She just had to endure for a little longer.

"Sweetie, please, you don't have to force yourself to continue living a life like this," Autumn said.

"I have no choice," Estella said, gripping Snow's hands tightly. "You know that the moment I say anything, Child Services will get involved, and they'll separate me from my sister."

Sister? Snow hadn't realized that Estella had a younger sibling. Was this why she was fighting so hard?

"I'm not saying that anything did happen, but if I did, Child Services would take her away from me. She's only seven years old, and I'm seventeen. There's no way that a family would take me in with her. She has more value as a child to be adopted than I do. I refuse to allow that to happen."

"Estella, I understand why you won't admit to anything, but this is no way to live. Unless you admit this to me, you and your sister will continue to suffer," Tanya said to her.

Estella was faced with an impossible choice: save her sister or stay with her. She couldn't have both.

"What does your father have to say about all of this?"

"I don't know," Estella said, gripping Snow's hand even tighter. "I haven't seen him in three years, ever since my mom cheated on him, and he cheated on her.

The only contact we have from him is the money he sends to keep her mouth shut about their relationship."

"Principal Tanya, please just let this go. I can handle it." Estella wanted to sound brave, but she was scared. Her only true family was her sister; she couldn't let her down.

"Estella, please." Snow couldn't bear to see her like this. She wanted to show Estella that she wasn't alone.

"Sweetie, there is no need to fear; we're here for you," Autumn told her. "I understand that you are afraid of losing your sister, but we will do everything in our power to help you."

"Estella, you must understand that, given your circumstances, even if you become an adult and start working a full-time job, you won't be able to take custody of your sister," Tanya said to her.

"You don't know that!" Estella yelled, refusing to believe that she couldn't save her sister.

"Estella, it's true. I experienced a similar circumstance when my parents died. Despite being twenty and having a full-time job, I was not allowed to take my sister Adrienne, who was thirteen at the time, under my care. I am sad to say that they won't ever let you take care of your sister."

"No, it can't be!"

Estella didn't want to believe it. Did all of her suffering account for nothing?

"There has to be a w-way," Snow said, embracing Estella, knowing that this was the best she could do to comfort her.

"Sweetie, I'm sorry, there isn't," Autumn told her. The best that they could do was work together with Child Services to make sure that the sisters remained close, even if they weren't together.

"Ahem, sorry to disturb you, but I think there is a way to solve both issues here," a woman with dark black hair said, bringing in a boy with brown hair who looked the same age as Snow and Estella.

"Vice-principal Adrienne, I'm sorry, but we are in the middle of an important discussion. I'm afraid that those who aren't involved in this matter need to leave," Tanya said to her.

I'm sorry, sister, but Nathan here has something that can help with your current predicament. However, I think it would be better to let him explain instead.

"Um, hi. I know this is sudden, but Estella, I'm sorry," he said, bowing his head to her. "I've actually known what your mother has been doing for a while now, and I was just too scared to do anything about it."

"Stop… don't," Estella didn't want him to say anything else. She didn't want to let them know. She didn't want people to look at her any differently.

"Estella, please. We're here for you," Snow said, being brave for her friend. "We… no, I want to help."

"Alright," Estella said. If Snow could be brave for her, she could also be brave. What mattered wasn't her, but her sister. She would do anything to keep her safe. "My mother abuses me. She… she does this…"

Estella couldn't think of the right way to explain everything she endured. All she could do was show it.

She took a hand wipe from the table in front of them, wiping off all the makeup on her left arm.

Everyone fell silent, staring at Estella's arm. It was covered in cuts, bruises, scars, and even burn marks. None of them wanted to believe what they were seeing. How could a girl this young endure so much?

"Estella?" Snow couldn't stop herself from crying. How was this fair? Estella didn't deserve this. She didn't deserve this pain.

"It's alright. Most of these aren't that fresh," Estella said, putting on a brave face.

"Estella, is… is the rest of your body like this?"

Tanya couldn't believe her eyes. She had dealt with abusive parents before, but never something like this. It was horrifying.

"Yes. Everywhere besides my face, which only has a few bruises," she said, pulling up her pant leg to show more injuries. "I hide them with my clothes, and what I can't, I hide with makeup. I got them when I disobeyed her or when she got drunk. I take my sister's punishments as well."

"Punishment? This isn't a punishment! This is torture!" Autumn yelled furiously.

"You don't have to suffer any longer," Adrienne said, placing her hand on Estella's shoulder. This girl had been through far too much; she deserved to be free.

"With your statement and wounds across your body, your mother will pay for what she has done. And even if she tries to weasel her way out of it, there is evidence that Nathan has."

"I'm… I'm sorry, I didn't think that it was this bad. If I knew I—"

"Stop," Autumn said to the poor boy. "You were scared. This isn't your fault."

"I'm sorry, I should have told someone sooner," he said, placing his phone on the table and playing a video of himself walking in the snow.

"Hey, what's going on, guys? It's your boy Nathan with another slice-of-life video! How do you all like the cold? Personally, I… huh? What's that... screaming?

The video moved from the snow over to a house that was all too familiar—Estella's. The window was closed, but muffled screams could be heard from the phone speaker.

"This is a bit creepy, isn't it?" the video Nathan said, getting closer to the window and looking inside. "What the heck?" he said in utter shock from what he was seeing.

"You stupid idiot! How dare you tell me what to do!" Estella's mother yelled in the video, smacking Estella across the face.

"B-but Stella needs food!" Estella cried out, holding her cheek.

"Then get it for her yourself! Your shitty father left you with nothing, so you'll get nothing! You should be grateful that I let you stay under my roof!"

"….."

"What the hell was that? You think that you have the right to talk back to me! You stupid idiot I'll—"

"Enough, that's enough," Adrienne said, pausing the recording and watching Estella begin to shake in fear. "The video goes on for another few minutes before Nathan stops recording."

"I… I never posted it anywhere. No one else knows. Please believe me," Nathan said nervously, ashamed of himself for never coming forward about this. He was afraid of what would happen to him, but now he was more convinced of his failure to help someone in need.

"We believe you," Tanya said, pleased that her student finally made the right choice. "Thanks to you, we finally have enough evidence to deal with her."

Chapter 15

"What the hell is this? Let me go! Do you know who the hell I am? I will sue you for this!" Estella's mother yelled as the officers led her out of her home.

"Ma'am, you have the right to remain silent…"

"You! I knew it was you!" she yelled, ignoring the officer reading her Miranda rights, focusing on the white-haired girl next to her daughters.

This all started a few hours ago after Nathan had shown them the video. Tanya and Adrienne wasted no time in calling the police and showing them all the evidence that they had: Autumn's eyewitness testimony, security footage from inside and right outside Tanya's office, Nathan's video, Estella's wounds, and her testimony. All of this was more than enough for them to get a warrant for Estella's mother's arrest.

Snow looked at Estella's mother as she struggled against the police officers. She never knew that such a person could exist. To do what she did to her own daughter made her nothing more than a monster.

"You and your mother are done! You will be ruined by this! Hear me! Ruined!" she yelled as the officers finally managed to shove her into the cop car.

"Excuse me, ma'am, but these two girls will have to come with me," one of the police officers said to

Adrienne, who had come with them to make sure that Estella would be safe.

"Big sister? Are they taking mommy away from us?" Stella asked, scared that her mother would come back and harm her big sister again.

"Yes, Stella," Estella said, kneeling to hug her sister. "She can't hurt us anymore."

"I know this probably isn't proper protocol, but these girls have been through far too much. Would it be possible for me to take care of them for the time being?" Adrienne asked them.

She didn't want to see two sisters separated, just as she and her sister were when they were younger.

"I'm her vice-principal; you can check my background if needed. I just... I don't think they need to suffer anymore today."

"Hmm, it's a very uncommon request, but since you are her vice-principal, having her spend a few nights with you shouldn't be a problem. However, there are several legal documents you need to sign, and this is only possible if they agree. Do you understand?"

"Of course. I would never try to bring harm to one of my students or their family," Adrienne said, knowing that the officer was pulling a lot of strings to let this happen. He could be seriously reprimanded for this as well, but just looking at the two sisters made him hesitant to separate them.

"Girls, are you all right about staying with Miss Adrienne for a while?" the police officer asked Estella and Stella, who nodded their heads simultaneously. They knew they were being given a blessing with this.

"All right, all three of you, please come with me to the station so we can complete the necessary paperwork."

"Are you alright?" Autumn asked Snow as they watched Adrienne leave with the girls.

"I'm…. sorry," Snow said, ashamed to look at Autumn. She thought she didn't care about Estella and was just like the people in her previous world. She didn't know if she had the right to say sorry.

"Sweetie, you did nothing wrong. I should have done better to make my intentions clear. I promise I won't ever make you feel that way again."

Snow and Autumn went home with a greater bond, preparing for the trial that awaited them.

For the next two weeks, Estella and Snow continued to go to school. Despite not living at home didn't mean that Adrienne would allow her to neglect her education.

It didn't take long for Ember to find out what happened, and she broke down in tears when she did. She hated that she hadn't helped Estella, but Estella made sure to let her know it wasn't her fault. Ember was her best friend, and that's why she never told her.

Aside from Ember, Nathan, and Snow, no one else at the school knew what was going on with Estella. This was to protect her from being targeted by the gossip of her peers.

However, there were still rumors circulating around the school about the crazy lady who attacked her, trying to blame it on Snow. Luckily, everyone understood that they were both victims and that the woman was the aggressor.

Within the first week following Estella's mother's arrest, everything had started to calm down. Now, after two weeks had passed, today was the day of the trial. Normally, things wouldn't be conducted this quickly, but after reviewing the evidence presented, the judge decided to hold a hearing as soon as possible. She would ensure that a monster who did such things to her own daughter would be punished.

"All rise for the honorable judge Abigail Turner! Today, we are reviewing the case of Estella Moon and Stella Moon vs Violet Moon."

Snow and Autumn were sitting behind Estella's seat, along with Stella, Adrienne, and Nathan. Tanya had to stay behind to maintain order at the school, but there shouldn't have been any problems. They would win this, and Estella would be freed.

Though Snow couldn't shake the thought that Estella's mother was up to something, despite having all the evidence they had against her, she looked fine and wore a confident expression on her face.

"The plaintiff may start," Judge Abigail said, beginning the trial.

"Your honor, my client, Miss Estella Moon, and her sister have been exposed to horrendous treatment for years," Mrs. Benson, Estella's lawyer, said during her opening speech. "Such treatment includes starvation, physical abuse, psychological abuse, and even torture."

"Your honor, her statements go too far!" Estella's mother's lawyer, Mr. Casey, shouted.

"Her statement will stand; wait your turn, counselor," Judge Abigail told him.

"Thank you, your honor. As I was saying, the treatment that my client and her sister have experienced is far too cruel for children their age. That is why, after carefully discussing with my client, we request that her mother give up legal custody of both her and her sister, as well as pay for her crimes."

"Very well, your opening statement has been heard," Judge Abigail said, allowing Mrs. Turner to sit down while Mr. Casey stood up.

"Your honor, my client and I are appalled by the accusations made by the plaintiff, and they simply aren't true. This is nothing more than a child's prank that has gone too far."

"A prank! Your honor, we have photographic and physical evidence of my client's damaged body," Mrs. Benson said, showing the stack of pictures in her hands. Not to mention, Estella was not wearing any makeup today, showcasing her wounds.

"While that outburst was uncalled for, it does help my client bring up another matter. I want to call my client up to the stand to give her testimony for the court to hear," Mr. Casey said smugly.

"Granted, you may proceed," Judge Abigail said, watching the woman confidently approach the booth.

"Mrs. Moon, do you solemnly swear that you will tell the truth, the whole truth, and nothing but the truth?"

"I do," she said, not even batting an eye, though everyone on Estella's side knew that she was a liar.

"Very well. Please proceed to give your testimony."

"Your honor, my daughter is not well. Ever since her father cheated on me, her mental state has been deteriorating. She starts to lose her mind and has fits of hysteria, causing her to harm herself. And if you know, I do have proof for the court: legal documents showing that she was seeing a psychiatrist, as well as proof of her being medicated."

"That's not true!" Estella yelled, fully aware that her mother used her name to obtain drugs for herself.

"Mrs. Benson, I advise you to keep your client quiet until it is your turn," Judge Abigail said while reviewing the documents presented to her. "As for you, Mrs. Moon, may we contact this psychiatrist to verify your claims?"

"I'm afraid we cannot. They recently retired and moved out of state, and they left no way to contact them," she said, delivering a blatant lie.

"Then I don't suppose you would object to the jury reviewing these documents themselves?"

"Of course not," she replied with a smile. She ensured that she paid a large sum to forge all these documents; there was no way some random juror could distinguish them from the real thing.

"Thank you for your cooperation," Judge Abigail said, returning Estella's mother to her seat before Mrs. Benson could give her rebuttal.

"Your honor, what my client's mother says is not true. My client has prepared video evidence of several events that can prove her mother was the aggressor. I shall present them now," she said, loading up the first video, which was the discussion they had in principal Tanya.'

".... I owe the two of you nothing. Not only do you waste my time, but you accuse me of something you have no proof of. I don't care about what you saw on Estella's face because you never saw how she got it. And more importantly, Estella will never tell you how she got it. So next time that either of you thinks about acting like a hero, don't. Stay out of my family affairs or else. I can have both of you put away for a long time, and Estella will help me do so."

"In this clip, you can clearly see that my client's mother is threatening the principal and the mother of a concerned parent for merely bringing up their concerns for my client. And a few minutes later, this event plays out," she said, switching to the following video.

"... See! Look at this! This unruly girl attacked my daughter!"

"Is this how the daughter of the friend of your principal acts? Is she allowed to harm other students because she thinks she has the power to do so? It's just like the girl who almost committed murder! This entire school is filled with problems!"

In this clip, you can clearly see my client's mother purposely creating a scene not only to put her daughter on public display, showing off her wounds, but also to insult a third-party student, accusing her of attempted murder.

And finally, the third and most crucial piece of evidence is the last video my client has prepared, given to her by a concerned classmate. I warn your honor and the members of the jury that the scenes in this video are quite disturbing.

"...You stupid idiot! How dare you tell me what to do?" Estella's mother, in the video, yelled, smacking Estella across the face.

"B-but Stella needs food!" Estella cried out, holding her cheek.

"Then get it for her yourself! Your shitty father left you with nothing, so you'll get nothing! You should be grateful that I let you stay under my roof!"

As you can see, your honor, this evidence proves that my client has been abused by her mother."

"Objection, your honor!" Mr. Casey yelled. "These videos were clearly taken without my client's knowledge! And they could have even been doctored!"

"Mr. Casey, the first two videos are from the school's security system. All footage recorded is sent to a main server outside the school's jurisdiction. As such, it could not have been altered in any way. As for the final video, you can say that the video has been doctored, but that means that you are willing to have it checked out by a specialist?"

"Your honor, the last video is a fake, not to mention that the person who took it was illegally trespassing on my client's property. They did not take this video out of the kindness of their heart. Besides, there is no reason even to suspect my client of abuse, given that during the time the video was taken, as indicated by the time stamp, she was auditioning to be an evil stepmother in a play. We have documented proof of all of this. My client was merely using her own daughter to help practice her role."

"As for the other two videos, while it is clear that my client's actions were not appropriate at the time, it is clear that she did everything to protect her daughter. We have proof of the actual culprit concerning the accusations against my client. Not to mention that she is in this very courtroom. Your honor, we would like to call Snow Dust to the stand."

Chapter 16

"Me?" Snow asked, nervous about being forced in front of a crowd.

"It's okay, sweetie. Nothing is going to happen." Autumn felt a bit worried about the situation, but the judge and the jury would have to be fools to believe that Snow could harm anyone.

"Miss Snow, if you would?" Judge Abigail asked as Snow slowly made her way to the stand.

She could see that Estella was anxious for her, while her mother's evil smile sent shivers down her spine.

"Miss Dust, do you solemnly swear that you will tell the truth, the whole truth, and nothing but the truth?"

"Y-yes. I do solemnly swear that I shall give the truth, the whole truth, and nothing but the truth," Snow said as Mr. Casey began his interrogation of her.

"Your honor, you may be unaware, as the rest of the court may be, but Miss Snow is not Mrs. Dust's biological daughter; she is, in fact, adopted. Though this wasn't from an orphanage, no, it was inside a hospital where she stayed for some time."

"After doing some research, I discovered that Mrs. Dust brought Snow to the hospital after she collapsed from hypothermia in front of her store. After taking her to the hospital, it was revealed that Miss Snow had lost her memories, along with any identifiable traces of who she was."

"Out of the kindness of her heart, Mrs. Dust decided to take her in. It's a heartwarming story—a girl with amnesia is adopted by the woman who saved her life. The kind of event you would see in a story."

"For that reason, I began questioning whether any of it was real. A girl with amnesia, whom no one has ever seen before, arrives in our town and integrates into a new family, no questions asked. I find it hard to believe."

"What if this whole amnesia act is nothing more than a ruse to draw suspicion away from herself? What if she is a dangerous criminal attempting to harm people in this town? My client has already stated that this girl harmed her daughter, which makes it clearer that she is dangerous."

"Counselor, I remind you that this is a courtroom, not a place where you can slander witnesses without evidence," Judge Abigail said to him.

"If you have something to ask her, ask it and then provide evidence for these claims you've made. If not, Miss Snow will be allowed to leave, and her name will be stricken from the record."

"Your honor, worry not; we have more than enough evidence to prove her guilt. I was merely offering this as a chance for the girl to tell the truth before it's too late."

"Truth?" Snow didn't understand what he was talking about. Why was he claiming she was dangerous?

"That's right, the truth!" Mr. Casey said, almost yelling at Snow. "Miss Snow, is it true that you lost your memories?"

"Yes."

"And is it true that Mrs. Dust saved you?"

"Yes."

"Now let me ask you, is this you in these pictures?" he asked, placing a photo of Snow holding a gun in her hand, along with several others of her stealing and harming people.

"That… that can't…" Snow knew she hadn't done any of these things, but why were there pictures of her doing them? Were they photoshopped?

"Miss Snow, answer the question," Judge Abigail told her. Seeing the pictures, she wondered how far this woman was willing to go to blame someone else for her crime.

"That… t-that is… me…" Snow didn't know what else to say. That was clearly her, but how? Was there something else she was remembering?

"You see! Under hard evidence, this girl has admitted to being a criminal!" Mr. Casey yelled as he handed copies of the pictures to the jury. "No one can vouch for this girl besides those who think she has amnesia. There is no telling what kind of criminal she is. Not to mention that these accusations against my client only emerged after she met this girl."

"Objection, your honor! How do we know if those pictures are even real?" Mrs. Benson yelled, furious that they would try to shift the blame onto a sixteen/seventeen-year-old girl.

"Really, then, what about this? Police reports of a white-haired girl robbing and killing an elderly couple in the state over? And this report of a strange white-haired girl lurking around several people's houses, watching their children sleep? And this one of a white-haired girl who was expelled for beating up and sending two of her classmates to the hospital."

"No! That's not true! She wouldn't do such a thing!" Autumn yelled, scared that they could prepare so much in the short amount of time they had.

There was no way that anything they said was true. She couldn't prove it, but she knew in her heart that Snow wasn't the monster they were trying to make her out to be.

"Mrs. Dust, stand down. One more outburst and you will be removed from this courtroom," Judge Abigail said to her.

She also wanted to believe in this girl, but the evidence was clearly stacking up against her. A trial where she was merely supposed to act as a witness was placing Snow in the spotlight.

"As for you, Mr. Casey, all evidence in this case will be thoroughly investigated."

"Of course," Mr. Casey said. "Though I doubt that will be necessary, seeing as each one of these was signed by three officers and had the proper stamp to show their legitimacy."

"If that is so, then there should be no problem checking again," Judge Abigail said to him. She knew that there was something suspicious about all the evidence they were providing, and she would ensure that the truth was heard.

"As you wish, Your Honor, we have a witness to prove that my client was targeted by Miss Snow from the very beginning. We want to call Alister Moon to the stand."

The doors of the courtroom opened, and the last person that Estella thought she would see appeared.

"Dad?"

The courtroom fell silent as Alister took Snow's place on the stand, allowing her to return to her seat beside Autumn, who was holding her tightly.

Autumn could feel Snow trembling with fear. How dare she accuse Snow of these things? This man had the power to either save or ruin Snow's life. What would he do?

"Sir, would you please state your name and your relationship to the defendant?" Judge Abigail asked, eager to discern which side he would take.

"My name is Alister Moon, ex-husband of Violet Moon and father of Estella and Stella Moon."

"Do you solemnly swear that you will tell the truth, the whole truth, and nothing but the truth?"

"I do, your honor," Alister said without blinking.

"Very well, counselor, you may question your witness."

"Thank you, your honor, and thank you, Mr. Moon, for arriving on such short notice. I know you are a busy man, being a famous magician. But I'll save the compliments for later."

"Mr. Moon, is it true that after your divorce, you agreed to give full custody of your children to your ex-wife with the condition of supervised visitation?"

"Yes."

"And why did you choose not to fight for custody?" Mr. Casey asked.

"Because I believed I was not fit for fatherhood," Alister replied, much to Estella's disappointment. "I love my daughters, but my constant traveling for work made it impossible for me to care for them properly. It was better for them to stay with their mother in a stable home. I made sure to provide for all their needs."

"Everything they could need, and a stable home. Now, I am sure it cannot be denied that my client provided just that. However, I am certain that you, Mr. Moon, are aware of the accusations against my client here, and you must know that she could never do such a thing. In fact, you are aware of the real danger to your daughters in this very courtroom."

"If you would, could you please present the evidence that will undoubtedly prove my client's innocence and show that Miss Snow has been targeting your family for years?"

"Do you mean the evidence that you provided to frame a child?" Alister asked, surprising everyone.

"M-Mr. Moon, I have no idea what you're talking about!" Mr. Casey exclaimed, looking nervous. "I'm sorry, your honor. Mr. Moon is known for making jokes during his performances. This must be one of them, right?"

"Your honor, I have not lied, and I do possess evidence to prove that everything I am about to say is true. However, I regret to inform you that none of it has been submitted in advance."

"You may proceed," Judge Abigail told him, allowing Alister's lawyer to enter the courtroom.

"Your honor, this is absurd!" Mr. Casey shouted in frustration. Alister was not supposed to present this evidence. "The witness just stated that none of this evidence can be properly used."

"Yes, while that may be so, he is your witness, yet he is denying your claims. Given the oddity of their submission, all documents and evidence they present will be thoroughly inspected. Mr. Moon, you may proceed."

"Thank you, your honor," Alister said, relieved to deal with an understanding judge. "As I mentioned earlier, all the evidence that Mr. Casey and my ex-wife wanted me to provide was fake. Here are receipts from well-known forgers using the card given to my ex-wife to support our children. All expenses on this card were meant solely for the children, and I can view all transactions made. Using it for personal matters violates our divorce agreement."

"Additionally, if you examine the police documents presented, you'll see they are dated over twenty years ago but have been made to look recent, not to mention that only one of them is authentic. The rest were falsified back then as well."

"My ex-wife contacted me through her lawyer in an effort to falsify evidence to blame this poor young girl. She intended for me to claim this girl as my illegitimate daughter to have a vendetta against her family, but that is not true, and I will submit to a DNA test if required. As for Estella, my ex-wife planned to lock her in a mental institution to avoid any guilt."

"Mr. Moon, the evidence you provided will most certainly change the jury's decision, but I must ask what your reasoning is for doing this?" Judge Abigail inquired.

"From what you say, your ex-wife expected you to side with her. Is there a reason for this?"

"Yes, your honor, this is," Alister told her. "It's because she threatened to reveal the affair I had while still married to her. This was another reason I gave up custody of my children. They did not need a father who could not stay loyal to the one they married in their lives. She wanted to threaten me to do her dirty work, but I couldn't do something like that to my daughter. Despite giving up custody of her and her sister, I will never stop loving them."

"Your honor, please! You can't listen to him! He's lying out of hatred for my client!" Mr. Casey yelled, sweating heavily.

"Enough!" Judge Abigail said, bringing down her gavel. "If no more witnesses or evidence exist, I will allow the jury to convene and decide their answer. May the truth come to light."

Chapter 17

A few days passed as the jury reviewed the evidence before they made their decision.

"We, the jury, find Violet Moon guilty of all charges against her, as well as the forging of evidence and trying to frame a minor."

"No! This isn't possible!" Violet yelled, looking over at Estella, who hugged her friends before her eyes landed on Snow. It was this brat's fault that everything was ruined.

"I hereby sentence Mrs. Moon to thirty years in prison," Judge Abigail said, happy that everything turned out for the best."

"You bitch! I'll kill you!"

Suddenly, in a fit of rage, Violet jumped out of her seat, charging straight for Snow.

But before Violet could get close to Snow, she found herself on the receiving end of a fist directly to her face.

"Don't you dare touch my daughter!" Autumn yelled, standing between them and looming over Violet, who was being grabbed by the guards.

"Let me go! Let me go! I'll ruin you!' Violet yelled, struggling to break free, but it was no use.

"No, you ruined yourself," Judge Abigail said, furious that a woman like this was allowed to walk free for so long. "For attempting to murder someone in this courtroom, I sentence you to life in prison. May you use this time to think about what you've done."

The atmosphere of the courtroom began to lighten as Autumn embraced Snow. She was safe, and this whole mess was finally over.

However, Violet refused to go quietly as she was being dragged away.

"You really think that skank is your daughter! None of you know who she is! None of you know what she is! But I do! I can't wait to watch you all burn!"

Violet laughed manically as she was finally pulled out of the courtroom. Everyone thought her words were nothing more than those of a crazy person, except for Snow.

Was Violet making all of that up, or was she actually crazy? Or was there some truth in her words? However, Snow didn't have the energy to deal with that right now. All that mattered was that Estella was finally free.

Although there was initial uncertainty about what would happen to Estella and Stella after the trial, there was actually nothing to worry about. Adrienne had decided to take them in as her own.

Alister declined custody of his daughters, realizing that he could never be the father they needed. However, that didn't stop Adrienne from ensuring that he would visit his daughters once a month.

Estella was very happy with this arrangement because she knew that she and her sister were safe. She no longer had to worry about their mother harming them ever again.

Ember was also pleased with this development because it meant she had two new cousins.

Snow was happy that Estella had finally found a place where she could be happy and heal.

The doctor mentioned that most of her physical wounds would fade over time, but she needed to be particularly cautious about the mental ones.

Estella endured much longer than most could bear. It would take time for her to fully recover, but she would be alright if her friends and new family stayed by her side.

Regarding Snow, one significant event occurred after the trial. Her relationship with Autumn became deeper, bringing them closer as a family.

"Snow! Hurry up! School starts soon!" Autumn yelled while Snow was busy locking a drawer in her room.

"Coming!" Snow yelled, rushing down the stairs and almost bumping into Lily.

"Hey, slow down!" Lily said, glad that Snow was doing much better these days. "It's only your second month of school. There's no rush."

"Sorry!" Snow said, smiling back at her.

Snow was excited because Estella had taken a leave from school after the trial and was finally returning today. She couldn't wait to see how she was doing.

"Calm down, sweetie. She's not going anywhere," Autumn said, handing Snow her lunch.

"I k-know, but I…"

"I know, sweetie, now run along. And here, make sure to share these cupcakes with your friends."

Autumn slipped a pan of cupcakes into Snow's backpack before she could even protest.

"Alright," Snow said, turning to leave for school, but she paused before turning around again.

"I love you, Mom!" Snow quickly kissed Autumn on the cheek before running straight out the door.

"…"

"Mom, are you alright?" Lily asked her mother, witnessing what Snow had just done.

"She… she called me Mom…"

Chapter 18

"So, how are ya'll liking your classes?" Allison asked Snow as they met up for lunch a few days after the trial.

Ever since they met before she started school, Snow has always had lunch with Allison. Lunch was divided into three different time slots at their school, and Allison was one of the few people she knew who shared the same lunchtime as her.

Snow enjoyed having lunch with Allison because she prevented crowds from gathering around them. Given everything that happened with Estella and her connection to Ember, Snow was quite the person of interest. Not to mention, she is still the new girl.

"It's good," Snow said back to her, opening up the lunch Autumn had made for her. "Gym is tiring, though."

Snow was doing well in most of her classes. The teachers were very nice, and they made everything easy to understand.

The only class she felt uncomfortable in was gym. Her body was far from strong, and her stamina was terrible. It didn't help that the same girl from her math class was trying to convince her to train with her.

"You have gym class with Alice, right?" Allison asked her. "She talks about you all the time. Says that you're like a newborn calf who can barely stand."

"Nggh…"

While it is true, Snow didn't like being compared to a baby. She needed to strengthen her body.

"I'm sorry. I was only teasing you. I didn't mean to upset you," Allison said, offering an apple as a peace offering.

"I mean to say that Alice doesn't mean any harm. She used to be just like you."

"Really?"

"Yes. She was even weaker than you are now."

There was no way that Allison was telling her the truth. Snow wouldn't be teased again.

"Here, if you don't believe me, check this out," Allison said, bringing out her cell phone.

Alice appeared on the screen. Her body was even skinnier than Snow's, making it almost miraculous that she was standing.

"This was taken back when we were in middle school. Alice was born with a weak constitution, but didn't let that get in her way. Little by little, she improved her stamina and became who she is today. It wasn't easy, but she never gave up."

"Really? You're not lying?" Snow wanted to believe her, but looking at the picture made it hard for her to see this person as Alice. She was so confident and strong. There was no way that she could have been this weak and timid like her before.

"Now, why would I lie to you? Though I won't force you if you don't want to," Allison said to Snow, aware that most people wouldn't believe this. "Though I will ask you to trust me."

"Don't worry, she's telling the truth."

"Estella!"

Snow's eyes lit up when she saw Estella sit down next to her. It was unfortunate that they didn't have any classes together, but they did share lunch, and that was more than enough.

Unable to hold back, Snow hugged Estella, both to comfort her and to comfort herself. Snow hadn't seen Estella that morning, so she was a bit overly eager to see her now.

She was so eager that she failed to notice the other students staring at them. However, Allison didn't let this go on for long.

"Hah! Your eyes lit up like the stars in the dead of night."

"Hmm?" Snow was confused. What was Allison saying while laughing at her?

"Sigh. I mean, you look pleased to see her. Happier than when you see me, at least. The only time I see you this happy is when you're with Ember."

"That's not t-true," Snow said nervously. While it was clear that she missed Estella, nothing special was happening here. She felt the same way when she saw Ember, too.

"Yeah, yeah. I can see that."

Allison could quickly tell that something was going on between them. However, she could also see the same vibe with Ember. Hmm, which one should she cheer for?

"Ugh, no need to say it in such a confusing manner. Snow is someone who cares about everyone," Estella said, denying Allison's implication, not noticing the saddened look across Snow's face as she did.

"Alright, if you say so," Allison said, dropping the subject as the three continued eating lunch. There was no point in pressing the issue. Things would work out in the end.

"On another note, how is it living with vice-principal Adrienne?"

"Well, it's…"

Estella spent the rest of lunch telling Snow and Allison what it was like to live with the vice principal and the principal. Surprisingly, she was more motherly than one would have guessed.

Once lunch ended, each of them went to their separate classes. However, Snow and Estella met up soon after classes were over, as today was the day they joined the pet welfare club.

"This is the place," Estella said, opening the door to the new club room, surprised to see a white bunny standing in their way.

"Mochi? What are you doing?" a pink and black-haired girl asked softly, picking up the bunny.

"Hmm? Two new members? Welcome, my name is Faye," she said, petting the bunny before looking at Estella and Snow.

Snow couldn't help but notice how much taller this girl was compared to her. Despite her meek personality, Faye looked taller than Allison and even Lily.

"Estella, it is so good to see you again. I'm sorry about what happened. If I knew I…"

"It's all right," Estella said, knowing that Faye had no malicious intentions. "I would rather not talk about it if you don't mind."

"I'm sorry; that was insensitive of me!" Faye said nervously. She understood that traumas like Estella's weren't easily forgotten, especially since they were still fresh in her mind.

"No, it's all right. It's kind of one of the reasons I'm here."

"You mean for the animals? Of course, having a bright and cheerful pet around certainly does help. What did you have in mind? Or would you like me to choose for you? Mochi here is one of the fan favorites of everyone who comes here. He is so cute and fluffy and doesn't squirm when you hold him. Do you want to give it a try?"

"I would love to, but I think he's more interested in Snow than me," Estella said, noticing that the rabbit was looking straight at Snow for some reason.

"Snow? Oh, where are my manners? It would be best if you were the new girl everyone is talking about," Faye said, realizing that she hadn't yet noticed Snow. The moment she looked at Snow, a sense of dread washed over her.

"It's you!" Faye yelled, sounding scared for a reason that Snow and Estella couldn't understand.

"You're the girl… the girl from the forest, who came out of the pond!"

"Wait? You were there?" Snow couldn't believe what she was hearing. This girl saw her come out of the pond when she first arrived here. Did she have answers to how she got here?

"Thank you so much!"

Before Snow could respond, she found herself being embraced by Faye. At first, she thought about breaking away from her, but for some reason, she couldn't bring herself to do so.

"Thank you so much for saving Mochi! When I went to the forest that day, he ran off. I chased him, only to find he was falling into the pond. I was too scared to jump in after him, but you appeared from the water, saving him."

"I wanted to thank you then, but when I tried to find you, you had disappeared. I never thought you would be the new girl here!"

"So, you don't know how I ended up in the pond?" Snow asked. She felt a bit disappointed that there were no clues about how she got here besides this bunny.

"You jumped in to save him," Faye said, looking confused. "I didn't see you jump in, but that's what must have happened. Do you not remember?"

"Snow has amnesia," Estella said, helping Snow sit down on the mat that was for the animals. "I heard from Ember that Snow doesn't remember anything after waking up in the hospital when Mrs. Dust found her.

"I'm sorry, you must have been so scared," Faye said, sitting beside Snow and grabbing her hand.

"It's all right," Snow said to her. It wasn't her fault that she knew nothing about how she got here.

Mochi began to nuzzle up to her leg as if asking Snow to pick him up.

"Aww, it looks like he likes you. Go on, pick him up. He won't bite," Faye said, encouraging Snow to feel the soft and fluffy bunny in her arms.

"He's… he's soft," Snow said, holding Mochi in her arms.

"I'm glad you like him," Faye said to her. "Sorry about this, Estella. I don't know if you wanted Mochi today, but since he picked Snow, would it be alright to choose a different animal? Thanks to the principal, we are allowed a wide range of animals here."

"That's fine. I'm more of a cat person," Estella said, smiling back at Snow.

"That's perfect! We have three cute kitties in the next room. Please come with me," Faye said excitedly, taking Estella with her to the next room.

Snow smiled. For someone who was supposed to be shy, she certainly wasn't when talking about animals.

"Hmm? I wish you could talk," Snow said, looking down at Mochi. "If you could, maybe you could tell me how I got here."

Snow wanted nothing more than to understand who she was. Did she have a life before waking up in the hospital? Were her memories nothing more than a figment of her imagination? And what about the evidence that Violet presented? Who was that girl, and why did she look like her?

"Huh?" Mochi began to tap Snow's hand with his paws. "Wait… do you understand me?"

Chapter 19

Mochi began to tap Snow's hand again, as if confirming her suspicions. He could indeed understand her.

"Can you… talk?" Snow knew it was stupid to ask a bunny this, but she couldn't help but do so.

"Of course, he can," Faye said, returning with Estella, who was holding a plump orange cat in her arms.

"He can?" Snow looked down at Mochi in awe. Could this creature talk?

"Yes, but not in the traditional way, mind you," she said, pulling out a laminated piece of paper with pictures. "Here, watch," she said, sitting beside Snow and Estella.

"Mochi, could you tell me what your favorite food is?"

Understanding Faye's words, Mochi jumped out of Snow's lap and placed his right paw over the picture of a carrot.

"Yes, I know that this way isn't very effective, but I still haven't found a better method yet," Faye said.

"It's amazing," Snow didn't know why Faye said it wasn't very effective. She was more than impressed by

Mochi's ability to understand them, as well as his ability to show what he wanted or knew.

"It really is," Estella replied. "It's not often that you see rabbits able to do this."

"Um, can I ask Mochi a question?" Snow asked, curious about what this bunny knew.

"Of course, you can," Faye said, happy to oblige. It was nice of them to let Mochi interact with them like this.

"Mochi, do you k-know where we first met?"

Mochi paused for a second before placing his paw over the picture of a glass of water.

"You remember." Snow couldn't believe it. It had been quite a while since she met him, yet this animal remembered where they met.

"Mochi has a perfect memory," Faye said, patting Mochi on the head. "Come on, let me show you what games he's good at playing."

They spent the next hour with the animals, playing and relaxing together. Snow could feel her stress beginning to fade away the more she played with Mochi, although she still couldn't fully relax.

She didn't know why she had never thought about going back to the pond before, but knowing that Mochi was connected to it made her unable to stop thinking about it. If she returned to the pond, could she go back to being who she was? But if she did, she would lose everything she had gained here: a family and friends.

Did she really want to risk what she had in her search for answers?

"Snow, are you alright?" Estella asked, noticing Snow staring out the window at the same forest where she had rescued Mochi.

It was fortunate that the pond was close to the school, or Snow would have been in trouble.

"Estella, I… I want to go back," Snow told her, making up her mind. She wanted to learn more, but she wouldn't do it alone.

"Back where?" Faye could tell that the moment Snow saw Mochi, she was troubled. She didn't know if she could help, but was willing to try.

"To the p-pond. I want to go back," Snow said, unable to stop trembling. However, she soon stopped when Estella placed her hand on her shoulder.

"Snow, you don't have to go back there," Estella told her. She couldn't stand seeing Snow scared and wanted nothing more than to protect her as she helped her.

Snow understood that Estella was worried for her, but she needed to be brave.

"I want to. Please."

"Alright, but I'll come with you."

"I will as well," Faye said to them. "I think it's safer if more of us go together."

Snow felt happy that her friends wanted to help her. With them by her side, she knew she had nothing to fear.

The three of them and Mochi soon left the club room, making their way toward the exit, but they quickly came face to face with someone unexpected.

"Estella, where are you going?" Vice-principal Adrienne asked, watching them try to leave the school. "Aren't you supposed to be in the pet welfare club?"

"I…" Estella couldn't think of what to say. She didn't want to worry Adrienne any more than she already had. There was no way they could tell her they were bringing Snow to the place where she almost drowned.

"I'm taking them outside for a bit," Faye said, thinking of a plan. "Outside activities and playing with animals simultaneously are very therapeutic."

"Really? Well, you are the expert. Just make sure that these two relax as much as possible. And Estella, make sure that you're back in an hour. We must pick Stella up from soccer practice and get dinner ready."

"Alright," Estella said back to her, blushing. She was embarrassed since she never had a proper mother figure in her life and didn't want her friends to see her being treated this way.

"Good, now you girls have fun," Adrienne said, returning to her office.

Snow couldn't help but let out a small giggle at Estella's relationship with Adrienne. It was clear that things were definitely getting better for her, and Snow was glad.

"Hey, what are you laughing about?" Estella yelled, embarrassed that Snow was teasing her. She had come a long way in the short time they had known each other. Friendship truly was a powerful medicine.

It didn't take them long to wake up from school and go to the forest, and with Mochi's help, they could find the pond with ease.

"Snow, are you alright?" Estella asked her, trying to ensure that Snow was okay.

"…"

Snow didn't answer Estella. She couldn't help but relive the memory of crawling out of the pond and making her way to Autumn.

"Snow? Snow? Can you hear me?"

Estella grabbed Snow and shook her gently to free her from her trance.

"We shouldn't have come here. I'm sorry. Faye, could you help… Snow?"

"The water… something is in it…"

"Snow? What are you talking about?" Estella asked, looking at the water and seeing nothing inside.

"S… ow… Sno… w… Snow…"

"Do you hear that?" Snow asked, hearing a gentle voice calling out to her, calling her name. For some reason, it felt… familiar.

"Snow, are you alright? Do you need to hold Mochi?" Faye asked, worried about Snow's pale expression. Trauma can easily manifest in places of significant importance to a person. It was clear that Snow shouldn't stay here any longer.

"Snow… come…"

"It's calling my name." Snow felt her body being drawn to the pond. She could see something glittering inside the water.

"Snow, we don't hear anything," Estella told her, knowing it was time for them to leave. Snow wasn't ready to be here.

"Snow… take it… take…"

Snow couldn't resist the voice, feeling increasingly compelled to grab the glittering object in the water. She needed to know what it was.

"What are you doing? Snow, it's dangerous to get closer than this."

Estella and Faye tried to stop Snow from moving any closer, but it was as if she were in a trance. She pushed past them and thrust her hand into the water.

Thankfully, all the snow had melted during Snow's time living with Autumn and Lily, but the water was still very cold. However, Snow didn't react to it at all. She seized what she saw glittering in the water and pulled it out.

"Yes… again…"

"Snow! What are you doing? You'll get sick doing stuff like that!" Estella yelled, bending down beside Snow to warm the poor girl's hands.

Why would she do such a thing? Was she trying to get sick?

"Here, hold Mochi. He'll warm your hand up," Faye said, forcing Snow to take Mochi out of worry.

While Snow accepted their help, she didn't respond to them. Instead, she was too enamored by the voice she was hearing to answer.

"You'll be... safe..."

"Safe?" Snow mumbled to herself, unaware that she was speaking.

"Of course you're safe."

Estella didn't understand what was happening with Snow, but she knew that staying here any longer wouldn't be good for her. "Come on, Faye, let's take her back," she said, helping Snow to her feet.

"Return... return to..."

"Alright." Faye agreed with her, taking the other side of Snow and leading her away from the pond, both unaware that something was still sparkling inside the water.

"Don't... go!"

Snow unconsciously tried to resist them, unable to fend off the urge of the voice, but Estella and Faye were too strong for her.

"Hmm? I thought you three just went out?" Adrienne asked, noticing the girls return to school so soon.

"Sorry, Snow got cold way too fast," Estella said, not wanting Adrienne to find out where they had taken Snow. At the same time, they had only been there for a few minutes. It had already taken a toll on Snow.

"We're going to warm her up with a bunch of animals."

"Alright, but if she gets a cold, you need to take responsibility."

"Don't worry, she'll be fine!" Estella yelled, not bothering to stop, leaving Adrienne to wonder what had actually happened.

They wasted no time bringing Snow back to the pet welfare club, where Faye brought out her fluffiest kitty, and Estella covered her with a blanket. But Snow didn't even respond; she kept staring at her clenched right hand, still holding whatever she had seen in the pond.

"Snow? Are you alright? …Snow?

"Re….. I… lo…"

"Snow!" Estella yelled at the top of her lungs, grabbing her by the shoulder and forcing her to wake up from whatever trance she was in, causing her to drop what was in her hands.

"Huh? Estella? W-what's going on?" Snow asked her, looking confused. "Weren't we just at the pond?"

"What? Do you not remember?"

Estella was shocked. How could Snow not realize that they had left the forest?

"We were, but suddenly, you started talking about hearing a voice, and then you stuck your hand into the pond, pulling out this," Faye said, holding up an ice-blue crystal necklace.

"What is t-that?" Snow didn't understand. Did she pull that out of the pond? Why didn't she remember doing that?

"You don't know?"

"No? Should I?" Snow asked, perplexed.

"No, it's fine," Estella said, realizing Snow didn't understand what was happening either. "We're just glad you're okay."

"That's right," Faye said, handing Snow the necklace. "While this necklace may be pretty, you shouldn't risk your health because of it."

Snow didn't know what to say. It was obvious that she had upset her friends, but she still couldn't grasp what had happened. Why didn't she remember anything?

The crystal felt cold in her hands as she fiddled with it. She had never seen a crystal like this before. What was it?

"Whatever happened, happened, but I don't think we should go back to that place again. It felt too risky."

Estella was right. Whatever happened to Snow back there could happen again if they returned. There was no point in going back if Snow might endanger herself.

"I'm sorry…" Snow felt upset. She didn't mean to cause problems for them.

"It's alright; you did nothing wrong. For now, let's call Autumn and get you home."

"Alright."

Snow did as her friends asked, waiting for Autumn to pick her up. But as she waited, she grew more and more curious about the necklace. What was it, and why did it feel familiar?

Chapter 20

"Get her!"

"Don't let her get away!"

"H-how? How did this happen?" the woman holding Snow asked, panting heavily as she ran through the forest. "How?"

Snow didn't understand what was happening. One second, she was in her room staring at the necklace, and the next, she was being carried away by a strange woman with white hair. All while black figures chased after them, screaming for them to stop.

She was too scared to move, let alone speak, as the woman continued to run. There was nothing she could do.

"Don't worry, sweetie, nothing bad is going to happen to us. It's all right," the woman said, navigating through the thickest trees to lose the men pursuing them.

Snow didn't understand why she felt comforted by this woman's words. Who was she?

It took some time, but the woman eventually managed to elude their pursuers for now, making her way to a familiar pond.

It looked just like the pond where Snow had fallen before. No, that couldn't be right. There was no way it was the same pond. She must be imagining things.

"There we go, sweetie. See? Nice and safe," the woman said, placing Snow on the ground and caressing her cheek.

Her hand felt warm and safe. It was a familiar feeling, but Snow knew this couldn't be real. The only people who would show her this level of affection were Autumn and her friends.

Snow tried to touch the woman's hand, only to realize that her hand looked like that of a child's. This only made Snow more skeptical about what was really happening, but again, she couldn't say anything.

"Sweetie. I need to go away for a while, and you need to stay here. Can you do that for me?"

The woman looked around nervously, ensuring no one was near, before pulling out the same necklace that Snow had found in the pond and placing it around her neck.

"…Good, I knew you could be a brave girl for me. Snow, sweetie, I need you to take this and keep it with you always. Hold on to this and never let it go. I need to take care of a few things before we can see each other again."

"Yes, I promise we will see each other again," she said, kissing Snow on the forehead, making Snow start to cry for a reason she couldn't understand.

"There she is!" one of the men chasing them yelled.

"Tsk, they found us faster than expected," the woman said, worried. The purple strands in her hair sparkled in the dim rays of the sun, distracting Snow from the horrors of what was happening.

"Don't worry, sweetie. I will return to you. I promise." The woman stood up, prepared to leave, but Snow didn't want her to go. Snow knew something terrible would happen if she did.

"Don't go!" Snow managed to yell, but it was already too late.

Before Snow could understand what was happening, she felt her feet leave the ground. The woman smiled at her, her face showing a sense of longing.

"Remember, I will always love you."

"Ahh~!"

Snow jolted up from her bed, gasping for air, believing she was drowning. Luckily, she realized she wasn't, but a small blue glint was visible from her right hand. It was the necklace.

Remembering everything she had seen in her dream, she threw the necklace across the room.

"No~!"

Unable to cope with what she had seen, Snow began to scream.

What was that? Who was that woman? Who was she? Why was she a child in that dream?

"SNOW!"

Autumn and Lily rushed into Snow's room after being awakened by her screams. Both were terrified by the state they saw her in.

The clothes she wore were torn, her room was destroyed, and she huddled in the corner, holding her knees to her chest.

"It's not real. It's not real. It's not real!"

Snow didn't realize it, but she was having a panic attack. Unable to cope with what she saw, her body began to wreak havoc on everything around her.

"Snow! Sweetie, it's okay. It's okay," Autumn said, trying to hug Snow, but her sweet words only reminded Snow of the woman in her dreams.

"No! No! Don't go!"

Snow continued to scream, unable to cope.

"Sweetie, I'm right here; we're right here."

Autumn didn't understand what was happening. Snow had been making such great progress. What caused her to act like this?

"It's okay, you're safe," Lily said, embracing Snow as well. It was heartbreaking to see the poor girl like this.

"No! Don't go! Mommy!"

Tears streamed down her face as Autumn and Lily continued to hold her. Neither of them let her go even after she cried herself back to sleep.

Chapter 21

"Tada! A slice of strawberry shortcake just for you!" Diana happily yelled, presenting Snow with a slice of cake.

After last night's events, Autumn had Snow take the day off from school. Neither she nor Lily could understand why Snow suddenly started to freak out like she did.

All they knew was that she needed rest. However, if it happened again, Autumn wouldn't hesitate to take Snow back to the doctor to get checked out.

She informed the school about Snow's absence and the reason for it. She tried to keep only the principal and the vice-principal in the loop, but since both were mothers of two students, it was hard to keep it under wraps. Estella and Ember told their friends what had happened to Snow, and each wanted to help in any way they could.

While they all wanted to visit her after school, they decided it was best if only two of them went so Snow wouldn't become too stressed. After a chaotic round of rock, paper, and scissors, the winners were Ember and Diana.

"Thank you, Diana," Snow said, accepting Diana's cake and laying it on her lap. She was too tired to eat.

After waking up from that nightmare last night and having a panic attack, Snow didn't get much sleep, even with Autumn and Lily's help.

They tried to get her to take some sleeping pills, but she refused. She didn't want to risk seeing that dream again. She didn't want to see that white-haired woman cry.

"Snow, you need to eat," Ember said, sitting down next to her and trying to feed her a piece of cake. "It's not healthy for you to do this to yourself. Your body is frail as it is. I don't want you to get sick."

"Ember, I—"

"No. Neither Diana nor I will listen to what you have to say until you agree to eat some of this cake."

"Yeah! I worked really hard on it. Do you really want it to go to waste?" Diana said, knowing Snow was too kind to overlook someone's hard work. It felt a bit unfair to guilt-trip her, but her health came first.

"Alright..." Snow couldn't say no to them, reluctantly opening her mouth so Ember could feed her.

"Good. Now, doesn't that feel better?" Ember asked, feeding Snow several pieces of cake before stopping.

"It's good."

"Of course it's good, silly! I'm the one who made it!" Diana said happily.

"Snow, remember that you need to eat or you will get sick, and you need to sleep as well. Those bags under your eyes are terrible."

While Ember was glad that Snow was listening to her, she needed to ensure that she would do these things without them.

"N-no… I can't… I won't," Snow mumbled, looking away from the girls. She refused to sleep.

"Snow, you have to. You don't want to worry, Autumn, do you?"

Snow knew she was only causing Autumn to worry by acting like this, but she didn't want to risk it.

"Can you tell us why you don't want to sleep?" Ember wanted to gain a better understanding of the situation. Snow wasn't the type of girl to act like this.

"That…"

Snow pointed to her desk, where the necklace she found yesterday lay. Autumn had discovered it while cleaning her room that morning.

"A necklace?" Ember was confused. How could a necklace make her not want to sleep?

"Wow, this is amazing! Where did you get this crystal?" Diana asked, taking it from Ember and examining it under the sunlight.

"Diana, do you know what that is?"

"Of course I do! Well, I don't know what it's called, but my sister is studying a crystal that looks like this at her university. She said the government asked her to study it because it has hidden properties. You know, stuff that can change the world and whatnot."

"Change the world? Diana, you're not on another sugar high, are you?"

"No way! I've only had three cookies and a slice of cake before coming here. I'm fine. Besides, have you ever known my big sister to make jokes? She's a geologist; she's as stern as a rock."

"Hmm, I won't deny that, but how did something your sister is studying for the government end up in Snow's possession?"

Ember was right, and Snow couldn't deny it. How could something this important be on a necklace?

"I… I don't know." Snow didn't understand. This had to be nothing more than a coincidence, right?

"Snow, it's okay. No one is accusing you of anything," Ember said, trying to calm Snow down as she noticed she was trembling.

"Here, if it makes you feel better, how about I take this away for a bit? Would that help you get some sleep?"

"No!" Snow stumbled out of bed, yanking the necklace away from Diana.

"Snow! Are you alright?" Ember asked, hastily picking her up with Diana's help, who was a bit startled by Snow's actions. The perfect cake she made was all over the floor. It was terrible.

"Y-you can't take it!" Snow didn't want her friends to be plagued by nightmares as well. She couldn't let them take it.

"Snow, please calm down."

Ember and Diana managed to get Snow back in bed, although she still wouldn't let go of the necklace.

"It's too dangerous," she said, trying to keep them away. However, the harder she held it, the colder her hands became, making it harder to grasp.

"Snow, we only want to help. Please tell us what we need to do."

"I… I don't know." Snow honestly had no idea what she wanted to do with the necklace, but she knew she couldn't let her friends take it. She didn't want them to experience this nightmare.

"That's fine," Ember said as she and Diana sat beside Snow. "Diana said that her sister is studying these crystals. Maybe she could help us."

It was a long shot, but if it could help Snow calm down, the Ember was willing to do whatever it took to help her.

"Really?"

Snow wasn't certain about that. Could she actually find answers with the help of Diana's sister?

"Of course, she can! Molly is the best of the best! You'll love her! And I just texted her while you were talking, and she says we can stop down today!"

Ember and Snow looked at Diana in awe. To think that she had done that before they even made a decision.

"Come on, what are we waiting for? Let's go!" she yelled, running out of the room to tell Autumn they needed a ride.

"Snow, it's alright. We won't leave your side," Ember said, placing her hand on Snow's to make her feel better.

"Huh? Snow was your hand always—"

"What this I hear about you going to college?" Autumn asked, interrupting Ember as she walked into the room.

In a quick second of embarrassment, Ember removed her hand from Snow's, forgetting what she was just about to ask Snow.

"Mrs. Dust, we thought it would do Snow some good to get out of the house for a bit. Diana's sister works at the nearby university, and she's invited us to check out her new research assignment."

"I don't know."

After what happened last night and Snow's current exhausted state, she didn't want her daughter to put herself in danger.

"Please." Snow looked at Autumn with baby-doll eyes. She knew she had caused Autumn to worry and didn't want her to continue feeling that way.

"Snow, I know you want to go, but I don't think I can allow it."

"Please, mom~."

Snow didn't want to use this tactic, but she felt she had no other choice. She remembered how happy Autumn had been when she called her mom for the first time, and realized she could probably convince Autumn to do anything for her by calling her mom.

"That isn't fair, young lady. Do you really think that by calling me mom, I'll do what you ask?"

"Um, ma'am, if you aren't going to take us, then why are you taking out your car keys?" Ember asked.

"I never said that I wouldn't take her, but that doesn't mean that she'll always get her way."

Autumn felt embarrassed. She hadn't even realized that she was taking out her keys before Ember mentioned it.

"If Snow wants to go to the university to see Diana's sister, she must first take an hour's nap and sleep on the car ride over. I will not take no for an answer, no matter how much you beg. Do you understand?

"Yes! Thank you!" Snow yelled happily, though she was still concerned about falling asleep, and Ember definitely noticed this concern.

"Snow, you might be worried, but I'll lay next to you the whole time. There is nothing to be scared of."

"Thank you," Snow said, feeling happy that Ember was by her side. Maybe with her next to her, she could actually get some much-needed rest.

"Good, and thank you, Ember. You two sleep well. I'm going to make some snacks for the trip with Diana. That girl is a master in the kitchen."

Autumn left Snow with Ember, knowing that she was in good hands, not paying attention to their blushing faces.

"I don't know a-about this," Snow said nervously. "She was happy that Ember wanted to stay with her, but she was now realizing that she would be left alone with a girl in her room.

"Don't worry about it, Snow. Just relax, close your eyes, and listen to the sound of my voice. That's it, relax. You're safe and tired—yes, very tired. You want to sleep. You want to rest."

"I… want… I want to sleep…"

Despite her initial doubts, Ember completely put Snow to sleep. Taking this opportunity, Ember removed the necklace from her, hoping that by doing so, it would help Snow sleep better.

Chapter 22

"Wow!"

Snow was in awe. The university was huge, and there were so many people walking around.

Thanks to listening to Autumn and taking a nap, Snow felt much better and was ready to meet Diana's sister and get some answers.

"Come along, Snow. We can check out the campus later," Autumn said, firmly holding onto Snow's hand as they followed Diana, who wasted no time bringing the four of them to her sister.

"And may I introduce you all to the greatest big sister in the world, Molly!!"

...

No one knew what to say at first. They had all followed Diana into this lab, only to find a girl with a blank expression on her face.

"Hello, Diana, it's good to see you…"

"Dang! Molly must really like you guys! She is usually never this expressive!"

Expressive?

None of them could tell what Molly was thinking. Though she didn't refute Diana's words, did that mean she was telling the truth?

"Well, Molly, my name is Autumn, and these two are my daughter Snow and her friend Ember," she said, greeting Molly.

"It's a pleasure," Molly said, responding in an uninterested tone.

"So, as you can see, this is what I have been asked to study," she said, guiding everyone over to a large clear container with a crystal twice Snow's size inside it. The crystal looked nearly identical to the one Snow found.

"As you may be able to tell, this crystal is unknown."

'What does that mean?" Ember asked, leaning closer to the container.

"Meaning there are no records of it anywhere. Its origins are unknown."

"They are?" Snow asked, pulling out the necklace, instantly catching Molly's attention.

Before Snow realized what had happened, Molly had already taken the necklace from her hands and scanned it under a specialized machine.

"How interesting… how is this possible?" Molly asked, studying the data that appeared on her monitor.

"Hey! You should have asked if you wanted to see it," Ember said, angry with Molly for going ahead and doing what she liked.

Snow wanted to ask for the necklace back, but she didn't have the courage to do so.

"Sorry, but… no way… where did this come from…"

"Sorry, Ember, just like how I go crazy with desserts, my big sis loves rocks. She can't stop herself when she finds one that she likes.

"No, that doesn't give her the excuse to take it away from Snow without asking."

"It's fine."

Snow didn't want to cause any issues, especially since they were the ones who came to Molly for her help. While she felt a bit nervous about letting someone else handle the crystal, she thought it would be okay if she didn't have it for too long.

"Snow, you shouldn't let people—"

"Here you go," Molly said, handing Snow the necklace back and interrupting Ember. "Sorry for taking it, but I needed to confirm something."

"It's alright," Snow replied. She knew that Molly didn't mean any harm. She was her friend's sister, and there was no reason for her to be worried around her.

"What was so important that you couldn't wait to ask for her permission?"

Ember had never met Diana's sister before, so she was still unsettled by her behavior.

"Because of this," Molly said, directing everyone to look at the monitor, which displayed two graphs.

"As you can see on the screen, the right graph represents the crystal given to me by the government, and on the left is the one on Snow's necklace."

"Um, I'm sorry, but I'm not too familiar with this; what are these graphs representing?" Autumn asked, struggling to understand what she was looking at, though she wasn't the only one.

"Both graphs illustrate the energy outputs of the crystals. As you can see, the graph on the right reads zero. There is no energy of any kind in that crystal. Conversely, the exact opposite is true for the crystal on Snow's necklace."

"For some reason, her crystal possesses an unusual energy that I can barely comprehend. It fluctuates as time goes by. The beginning of the graph indicates the crystal's energy right after it left Snow's hands. After a few seconds, it becomes apparent that the energy is decreasing. The change is slight but still noticeable. However, based on the graph, I can tell that the crystal can retain this energy level for days, even weeks."

"Now, Snow, if you would, could you please hand me back the crystal?"

"Okay," she said, intrigued by what Molly was saying.

"Thank you. Now, look at this." The graph began to change, and then the slight energy the crystal had lost returned.

"I don't know how to explain this, but there is a way for me to test the theory I'm considering," she said as the glass container surrounding the giant crystal rose up. "I would like all of you to step forward and touch the crystal, with Snow being the last one."

"Are you sure we should be touching something like this?"

Autumn wasn't sure if it was safe to touch. Not to mention, the government gave this to Molly. Are they allowed to touch it? And if they aren't, will they get in trouble?

"It's alright. I decide what can and can't be done with the crystal. Please go ahead.

Listening to Molly's instruments, they each touched the crystal individually, but nothing happened. When it was finally Snow's turn, she hesitated for a moment. She felt scared, almost as if she knew what was about to happen next.

The instant Snow touched the crystal, she sensed a wave of cold energy wash over her body, and then the crystal began to glow.

It started as a dim light, slowly growing as the seconds passed, and so did the graph. She couldn't hold onto it for long as Molly pulled her away. When her hand left the crystal, Snow felt strangely tired.

"Hmm, it's just as I thought, Snow is…"

"Sir, are you seeing this? The energy in the crystal is rising!"

"Yes, I am. Finally, after all these years, it will be ours…"

Chapter 23

"I don't understand," Autumn said to Molly.

"It's like I said, I need a blood sample," Molly replied, preparing a small syringe. "I don't know why, but for some reason, the crystals react to Snow, and a strange energy can be found in them afterward."

"I'm weird?"

Snow didn't understand. There was no way she could be special, but what if there was something… no, that was impossible.

"Not necessarily," Molly reassured Snow. "The fact that the crystal didn't respond to anyone but you is most likely just a coincidence. But if I have a blood sample, I could determine the conditions necessary for the crystal to begin absorbing the energy. I only need a small sample. So what do you say? Are you willing to help?"

"You most certainly will not!" Autumn exclaimed, refusing to let Snow give up her blood. "Sweetie, your body is weak as it is. I don't want you developing anemia because of this."

"Don't worry, Mrs. Dust, it'll be fine," Diana said, knowing her sister would never try to harm one of her friends.

"I want to do it," Snow said. She wanted to know what was happening here and, if possible, find out why she came here.

"Snow, sweetie, you don't have to." Autumn was scared for her. She didn't want her daughter to be put in harm's way.

"Please." Snow didn't know of any other way to convince Autumn besides begging her.

"Fine, but you are eating a lot after this," Autumn said, giving in.

Seeing that she had permission, Molly wasted no time injecting Snow with the syringe and drawing some of her blood.

While the amount that she took wasn't much, Snow still winced as the needle pierced her arm. She never liked needles for that reason.

"There, all done," Molly said, already getting more equipment ready. "Diana should know the way to the cafeteria. You should be able to get something to eat there."

"What? Molly, you're not coming?" Diana asked, sounding disappointed.

"I can't; there's too much to research."

"I understand that you are invested in this, but there are times when you need to relax. Come on, don't you want to spend some time with your sister who came here to see you?" Ember asked her.

"Didn't you come here to see the crystal?"

"What? No way. I came to see you! They came to see the crystal," Diana said, hugging her sister.

"Fine, but I can't stay for too long." Molly knew that she couldn't refuse her sister. And besides, she could use a break.

Seeing that Molly had agreed to eat with them, Diana happily led them to the cafeteria.

"Snow, stay close, alright… Snow?"

Snow had followed Diana out of Molly's lab like everyone else, but before she knew it, she got lost in the crowds of people all around them. She had no idea where she was and had left her phone in the car.

She had never been around so many unfamiliar people without someone to support her. She couldn't do this. She needed a place to take a break.

Snow found herself drifting away from the crowds into a secluded area where she could catch her breath. If she stayed here, Autumn and the others would come looking for her. All she needed to do was… wait, what is that?

Snow's eyes landed on a display filled with class pictures of what looked like a research team. At first, there was nothing for her to notice, but it was then that she saw her: the woman with white hair.

It was her; Snow was sure of it. The picture from the trail and the image of her from her dream were the same. She couldn't get any closer because of the glass, but she could tell this woman looked just like her. The only difference was the purple highlights at the end of her hair instead of blue.

"Who are you?"

The voice would not stop, practically, *"I love you."*

"Nggh!"

The woman's voice from her dream echoed in Snow's mind, causing her to wince.

"N-no… please no…."

She didn't want to relive that dream again. She had to—

"I love you. I love you. I love you. I love you. I love you. I love you. I love you. I love you. I love you. I love you. I love you. I love you. I love you. I love you. I love you."

"Nghhh! No! Stop! Stop it! Stop it, please!"

"I love you. I love you. I love you. I love you. I love you. I love you. I love you. I love you. I love you. I love you. I love you. I love you. I love you. I love you."

The voice would not stop, and she practically screamed inside her head. She wanted it to stop; she wanted it to…

"Are you alright?" a girl asked, placing her hand on Snow's shoulder.

The moment she did, the voices finally stopped, leaving Snow alone. When she turned around, she saw a girl no older than herself with frizzy black hair standing before her.

"Th-thank you, I'm fine," Snow said, slowly backing away from the girl. "I was just…"

"It's alright; I sometimes get like that, too. I'm like, argghh! And nooo! You know, stuff like that…"

Snow couldn't help but let out a small laugh. This girl was awkward like her. It made her feel at ease with her.

"I'm—"

"Excuse me? Are you Snow Dust?" Two security guards approached the girl, interrupting her before she could introduce herself to Snow.

"Yes?" Snow didn't know why, but she felt uneasy around these two. They looked at her in a strange way.

"That's great. Your mother is looking for you. Come, we can take you to her."

"She's looking for me?" Snow asked, happy that Autumn was searching for her.

"Yes, now come with us, and we can take you to her," they said, eagerly urging Snow to come with them.

"Wait, I don't think that you should go with them," the girl said, holding onto Snow's hand.

"It's alright."

Snow tried to reassure the girl that they would only take her to Autumn and that there was nothing for her to fear.

"Are you two done? Your mother is eagerly waiting for you. Stop wasting our time."

Huh? Why did their tone suddenly change? Snow didn't understand. Could they be trusted?

"What the hell are you doing? Let's go."

What? How could they act like that toward someone they're trying to help? Snow wasn't entirely sure, but she could tell these guys were bad news.

"Sorry, but she just texted me to meet h-her at the car. I think I can manage."

"Really? She just texted you?" one of the men asked, blocking the path Snow was looking at. "Let me see the message."

"No! Y-you can't force her!" the girl yelled, stepping between them, to their confusion.

Snow had no idea what was happening. Why were they trying to force her to go to Autumn?

"That's it; I'm not playing Mr. Nice Guy. You're coming with us!" the man yelled, pushing the girl aside and roughly grabbing Snow's wrist, yanking her toward him.

Snow screamed, feeling as if her arm would be torn off.

"Let me go!" she screamed, unable to hold back her tears.

"Ugh, can't you keep her quiet?" the other man asked as the first began dragging Snow away.

She squirmed and screamed for help, but there was no one around to hear her except the girl, and there was no way she could help against two men who were twice their size.

"I'm trying, but she won't stay still."

"No! Stop it!" Snow screamed, scratching at the man's hand with her nails in an attempt to escape.

"Just shut up already, you—"

"Let her go right now!" Autumn yelled, running toward them as fast as she could.

She had been desperately searching for Snow after realizing that they had been separated. She didn't want anything bad to happen to her. To her shock, though, she was too late.

"Ma'am, you need to back away. We are bringing this girl back to her mother. Don't interfere," the man holding Snow said, squeezing her wrist tightly to keep her from talking.

"I'm her mother!" Autumn yelled, smacking the man across the face, allowing Snow to wriggle free from the man's grasp.

"You!"

The man grabbed Autumn by her collar, lifting her into the air.

"Who the hell do you think you are? You'll pay for-argh~!"

The man dropped Autumn, who had just pepper-sprayed him directly in the eyes.

"Stay back! Get on your knees!" Autumn yelled, determined not to let the men who tried to kidnap her daughter escape.

"Ma'am, put that down. There's no need for violence," the second man said, attempting to move closer to her while the other man knelt, rubbing his eyes, trying to wipe away the pepper spray.

"No! I refuse to listen to those who would dare harm my child. I've already contacted campus security. You aren't leaving here.

"Sigh. This is why I said that we should have waited for her to be alone so we could have just knocked her out, but this idiot insisted on doing the fake security guard act," the man said, talking to himself.

"It's fine, it's fine, that's why I made sure to come prepared. Take the girl."

The girl screamed as another man came up behind them, throwing her to the ground and grabbing Snow.

"No! Let me go!"

Snow struggled and squirmed against the man's grip, but he refused to let go.

"Snow! Let her go!" Autumn yelled, furious that they would dare use such an underhanded tactic. She couldn't get close enough to pepper-spray him without harming Snow.

"Mom!"

Snow was scared. Why was this happening to her? Was it because she was asking around about the crystal? It wasn't fair. All she wanted was to live in peace with her family.

"Ugh! What the hell?"

For some reason, the man holding her started behaving oddly; the tips of his fingers slowly became cold, and within seconds, so did his hands.

"What are you doing? Take the girl away now!"

Snow didn't understand what was happening, but she could feel the man's grip on her loosening. This was her chance. Using all the strength she had in her hand, she broke free from the man and tumbled to the ground.

"What the hell are you doing?"

The second man was confused. Why wasn't his partner moving? It was almost as if he were frozen.

"I'll get her," the man who was pepper-sprayed said, slowly rising to his feet. He could barely see, but it was more than enough for what needed to be done.

"No! You-agh~!"

The first man smacked the bottle of pepper spray out of Autumn's hands, knocking her to the ground.

"Mom!"

No, no, no. Why? Why did this have to happen? Why did Autumn have to suffer?

"Stay right there, you little pest!"

The man who was pepper-sprayed tried to grab Snow, but jerked his hand back as if he were in pain.

"What the hell is your problem? Why can't you idiots do anything right?" the second man yelled, approaching them.

"No! Stay away!"

Snow was scared. She wanted this to end. She wished for it to be nothing more than a bad dream.

"Come on! We have to go!"

Suddenly, the girl grabbed Snow's wrist and pulled her to her feet before running, leaving Autumn behind.

"Mom! No! We can't leave her!" Snow yelled, unable to break free from the girl's grip.

"She'll be fine! They don't want her!" the girl yelled, ignoring Snow as she led them outside. "We have to get you somewhere safe!"

Chapter 24

"No! We have to go back!" Snow yelled, trying to run back, but the girl wouldn't let her. It was too dangerous. "We have to help her!"

"No, you don't!" the girl yelled, nervously looking around.

They were making their way through the dark campus. Not many people were walking around, but it was enough to keep them hidden in plain sight for a few minutes.

"What I mean to say is that you don't have to worry, and, um… she'll be fine."

"Why? Why is this h-happening?"

"It'll be fine… she… I mean… I guarantee… um, let's keep moving," the girl said awkwardly, making Snow even more nervous than before.

"No…"

"What was that?" the girl asked innocently, but Snow realized something was amiss. This girl had shown up just before those men. How could she be sure that this wasn't a trap?

"I can't trust you. I have to go back!" Snow tried to run away, but the girl was much faster than she appeared. She blocked Snow's escape.

"Please! I don't want to harm you. I want to help!"

"No! You lie! Everyone lies!" Snow couldn't hold back the panic attack that was swelling inside her. After being assaulted by those men, witnessing Autumn getting hurt, and being dragged away by this girl, she simply couldn't handle it.

"No, I… I was just scared, yeah! I didn't know what to do, and, um, I grabbed you by accident! I'm sorry!"

The girl's words sounded suspicious, yet they unexpectedly helped Snow calm down. This girl was just as frightened as she was.

"I have to go back." Snow knew she had to be brave and return to Autumn, but what could she do if she did?

"No, you can't. We, uh, have to keep moving. We can find help for her."

The girl made a good point. Snow wanted to save Autumn, but what could they possibly do against those men?

"Come on, we're almost there," she said, grabbing Snow's hand once more and pulling her along.

Snow felt terrified. What had they done to Autumn while she ran? If she were hurt, Snow would never be able to forgive herself. But she knew Autumn wanted to keep her safe. There was, huh?

Suddenly, the girl stopped. Five guys in basketball shorts and tank tops with Oakley sunglasses perched on their heads blocked their path.

Snow's heart raced as though it might burst from her chest. She hid behind the girl, fearful that they were with the men pursuing them.

"Back off!" the girl yelled, attempting to sound brave, but her trembling body betrayed her fear.

"Woah, woah. It's okay."

"No one is thinking of harming you.

"We would never touch anyone without their consent."

"We just saw that you both looked distressed and were wondering if you needed help."

"Though we aren't saying this because of your apparent gender. We are saying this because we wish to help."

"If you don't want it, we will back off right now."

"We will not force you to accept our help; we are just letting you know that we are offering it."

These five guys were the embodiment of PC culture, or at least what they tried to be. They were precisely what Snow and this girl needed.

"Please! We need your help!" the girl yelled desperately to them. "There are creepy men dressed as security guards chasing us! They hurt her mother! Please!"

"What? Some people are attacking innocent women? We can't let this stand! Show us where they are, and we'll ensure they learn what it means to mess with the PC Bros!"

Snow couldn't be happier. She didn't know if they wanted anything in return, but she was willing to pay whatever it took to help Autumn.

"Thank you so much! They are down that way. They are dressed just like security guards." The girl tried to leave with Snow, but the PC Bros wouldn't let them pass.

"What are you doing? Giving us a direction won't help. If you want us to help, then you're going to need to—"

"What the hell! Brad! Wake up, buddy!"

Suddenly, the one speaking fell face-first onto the ground. Snow felt her body begin to tremble as she turned around to see the three men from before approaching them.

Snow's heart sank when she didn't see Autumn among them. Was she alright? Was she safe?

"No, we have to go... agh!"

The girl started to stumble, barely able to stand without Snow's support. A small dart was poking at the side of her neck.

"You! What did you do to Brad?" yelled one of the PC bro's at the approaching men, but just like Brad and the girl, he and the others were soon struck in the neck with a fast-acting tranquilizer dart. "You…"

"Ugh, finally," said one of the men, kneeling down to Snow, who lacked the strength to keep the girl standing.

"I hate colleges. They are all filled with annoying trash like this. I almost hate them as much as this brat: they only cause more problems for me. My job was supposed to be simple. Take you discreetly and return, but you didn't want to come quietly. Now, look at the results of your actions. None of these people had to get hurt if you hadn't resisted in the first place."

"Mom?"

"Hmm? Do you mean the one who pepper-sprayed one of my men? She's alive, but she'll know now not to mess with people like us."

"So, little lady, I'll be nice and give you a choice. You can either come with us willingly, or we can take you by force. Oh, and to ensure that no one gets in our way, we'll make sure to exterminate everyone here who saw us.

"No..." He couldn't be serious, could he? Would he really kill them because of her?

"Oh yes, and to make you understand who's in charge, I'll make you watch one by one as the life leaves their eyes. I think that will do nicely, don't you?"

"No! I'll go! Please, don't hurt them!" Snow yelled, scared out of her mind. She didn't want these people to be killed because of her.

"Good, now get up!"

The man forcefully brought Snow to her knees, dragging her away.

"G-got to find her. Please be safe," Autumn said to herself, limping toward the sound of police sirens.

She had just woken up after being knocked unconscious by those men. Her body ached all over and was covered in bruises, but she didn't have time to worry about that. What mattered was finding Snow.

"Please... help, I need your help," Autumn stumbled toward the closest officer, falling into her arms.

"Ma'am, are you alright? What happened? Who did this to you?" the female police officer asked her, observing the bruises on Autumn's body.

"My daughter, please, where is she?"

"Your daughter is missing? Did she have white and blue hair?"

"Yes."

"Ma'am, based on the testimony from these five young men who were attacked not too long ago, I'm afraid that your daughter may have been kidnapped."

"No…" Autumn couldn't bear what she just heard. Snow was gone because she failed to protect her.

Snow winced as she was blinded for a moment by the light being shoved against her face.

"How the hell did you do it?" the man on the other side of the table asked.

After she was taken away, these men tied her up and blindfolded her. Before she knew it, she was being shoved into this room and interrogated by this man.

"What?"

She had no idea what he was talking about.

"Don't play dumb with me!" he yelled, banging his hands on the table. "How did you get the crystal to work?"

"The crystal?"

"Really? Trying to play dumb when we found this on you."

The man threw the necklace onto the table in front of Snow. As she reached for it, he prevented her from grabbing it.

"That's mine!" Snow yelled, refusing to be bullied by these people after what they did.

"So what? Do you realize that this is our property, not yours? It belonged to us long before you were born, just like the one we gave to that girl at the university to study. We don't know how you got this, but we do know that you have the ability to activate them! How did you do it?"

"I don't k-know. I can't help you."

"Still going to keep hiding the truth? I tried to do this the nice way, though I'm glad that I get to do it the hard way."

Snow screamed as he grabbed her hair, yanking her towards him.

"Answer me!"

"I don't know!"

Tears began to flow from her eyes from the pain of her hair being pulled and the fear she was experiencing.

He didn't even try to be nice in the first place. He wanted to hurt her from the being. He was only giving himself an excuse to do so. He was a monster.

"Stop lying! I will kill everyone you love unless you tell me the truth! I'll—"

"What the hell is going on here?" A man dressed similarly to the one harming Snow yelled, storming into the room. "Release her this instant!"

"But sir—"

"I said now!"

The man holding Snow released her as commanded, but this was just the beginning of his reprimanding. He knew he had messed up when he touched Snow, but it was already too late.

"What the hell were you thinking? You were told to interrogate her. That means asking her questions, treating her respectfully, and calmly talking to her! That doesn't mean yelling, threatening, and resorting to physical violence because you think you can get results that way. We follow protocol here!"

"But sir, I—"

"Quiet! I don't care what you have to say. Report to Room D. You're done."

"Yes, sir," the interrogator said to the man, slowly leaving the room while scornfully gazing at Snow.

"I am terribly sorry for how he treated you. Are you alright?"

Hmm? Why was this man being nice to her? Was this that good cop, bad cop thing that she'd seen on TV?

"I'm f-fine," Snow told him, taking a few steps back.

"I'm sorry that things had to happen this way. The director was so excited to meet you that they failed to inform the people who brought you here and the man from before to treat you with respect. Please, if you would, the director would like to have a word with you."

The man opened the door and signaled for Snow to leave. He made it seem like she had a choice, but there was only one: do as he said or face the consequences. So Snow obeyed.

Out in the hall, the walls were black, and everything seemed clean. It was the suspicious kind of clean where you could tell that something sketchy was happening behind each door. The room that Snow left was labeled Room I.

"Don't bother looking around," the man told her, leading her to an elevator. "You won't be coming back to this floor."

He pressed the top button, and the elevator went up.

Snow wanted to ask this man questions, but she was too scared to talk to him. She just wanted to go home. Home to where Autumn and Lily were. Autumn got hurt because of Snow. Could she ever forgive her?

"We're here," he said as the doors opened, revealing a fancy office space. "She's waiting for you."

Before she could even think about stepping inside the room, the man shoved her out of the elevator, closing it behind her.

"Come, sit," a woman said from behind the chair next to the window.

Snow did as she was asked, slowly making her way over to one of the sofas in the middle of the room and sitting down.

"Who are you?" Snow asked, unable to see who was behind the chair.

"The better question is, who are you?" the woman said, spinning the chair around.

The woman was an older lady. Wrinkles were hardly visible on her face, and her hair was completely white. She wore a suit and held herself with great poise.

"To think that I would find you after all this time. It's quite curious that it took this long."

She walked over to Snow, sat beside her, and lifted her chin.

"What?"

This woman was talking as if she knew Snow, but that was impossible, right? She wasn't from this world. There was no way anyone could know who she was.

"So shy and cute. You're so different from the last one. She was a pain to deal with, but I can see that you will be much easier to use. You have so much more potential than the last one ever did."

"What are you talking about?" Snow asked, frozen in fear.

Why was this woman looking at her like an object?

"I can see that you're scared, but there is no longer a reason for you to be. Everything here is for you. We need your help. Please say yes. There is no way we can do this without you."

Chapter 25

"Who are you?" Snow asked, trying to move away from the woman.

"Really? Again, with that question?" the woman asked, sounding annoyed. "I've been searching for you for the past fourteen years, and you still don't understand who I am?"

"Fourteen years? No, I'm not... I'm not from here."

"What? You're not from here?"

The woman asked in a sarcastic tone.

"I can't be who you're looking for, I'm... I'm nobody."

"It's cute that you think that. But you definitely are the one I've been searching for. Your DNA is an exact match to what it was fourteen years ago. Not to mention that you can't hide the family trait."

"What?"

What was she talking about? Family? Snow looked up at the woman and noticed that near the ends of her white hair were purple and blue strands, resembling those of the woman in the picture.

"Do you realize it now? You and I—we're connected; we're family," the old woman said to her with a smug grin.

"No…"

"Oh yes, fourteen years ago, you were taken from me, and you somehow managed to stay hidden from me all this time. That must be more of her doing. She was always getting in the way."

"No! You lie! You lie, you lie, you lie!" Snow yelled, trying to remember her past and what she was doing before she met Autumn, but her memories felt lost—just like… just like a dream.

"No…"

"I do wonder where you've been this entire time," the woman said, standing up and walking over to a board. It was filled with pictures of Snow from the day she first arrived at Autumn's, meeting Ember, going to court for Estella, and even some from today.

"How you were able to remain hidden for fourteen years is no small feat. No matter, all that matters is that you have returned."

"I want t-to go home," Snow said, refusing to listen to this woman, no matter what she claimed. She was nothing more than a con artist trying to trick her, right?

"Home? No, no, no. You won't be going back to that person. You belong here with me, and I have no intention of letting you go."

"You see, this crystal is the exact one found on your necklace, or rather, my necklace," she said, pointing to the one on her desk. Stolen from me fourteen years ago, and it's finally returned to its rightful owner. However, it matters little now that we have found even more. You must have seen the one that we sent to the university. That was only a small sample of what we've already collected.

"I can't wait to begin the experiments again. There is so much that was abruptly left off after the previous… no, that one doesn't matter anymore because you're here now."

"Experiments?"

The way the woman looked at Snow sent chills down her spine. She felt frightened. She didn't want to be here. She just wanted to go home.

"Precisely. I did say before that everything here is for you, and that's no lie. You possess a connection to these crystals, and just like the previous subject, we need you to help us harness this connection. This is why you are here."

"I don't want to!" Snow yelled, trying to be brave. "I want to go back home!"

"Again?" the woman asked, grabbing the bottom of Snow's chin and pressing her thumb and index finger against Snow's cheeks to keep her from talking.

"Your home is here now. You will help us with these experiments, and we will do great things here. We will change the world. No one will come for you, and even if they did, they won't get close enough for it to matter."

"You will be well taken care of during your time here. Everything you could ever want will be provided. You'll live a far better life here than being the adopted daughter of some old bookstore."

"Trust me when I say that you will love it here, and you will never want to leave. Do I make myself clear?"

Tears started flowing from Snow's eyes, realizing she would never see Autumn, Lily, or any of her friends again. She should never have tried learning about that crystal."

"I asked if I could make myself clear."

"Yes…"

"Good!" the woman said in a perkier tone, allowing Snow to crumble to her knees. "Oh, and from now on, when we meet, I want you to call me grandma~."

Chapter 26

"You can take her now. She'll need a bit of rest before we start," Snow's "grandmother" said, pressing her intercom.

Seconds later, several men entered and dragged Snow with them to the elevator. She didn't even bother to resist, as she was still trying to wrap her head around everything she had just learned.

Her grandmother sat back down, soon receiving a video call on her computer.

"So, I see you like my gift," the caller told her.

"Gift? You didn't give me anything," she responded. "I'm the one who found her and brought her back here. You did nothing."

"My dear Winter, you truly were never one to see the big picture of things now, were you?"

"Don't you dare insult me! I'm the one who has both the crystals and the girl. Things will continue the way that I deem them to."

"Of course, the board would never want to impede your research. All I'm saying is that you underestimate the influence we have. You may have found the girl and brought her back into the fold, but do you think it's just a coincidence that she was found now, right when we discovered more of these precious crystals?"

"You can't mean that you planned this."

"Let's just say that we have our own ways of finding things, as well as releasing them."

"Still hiding things from me after everything that I have sacrificed for this research? Care to explain why I continue this partnership with you?"

"If you get rid of us, there will be no one left to cover for your mistakes. You do remember what happened to the last test subject, don't you? We wouldn't want another repeat of that now, do we?"

"Of course not," Winter told them, furious that they would dare bring up what happened to the last test subject.

"Very good. Just remember to focus on your experiments; we can do the rest. The board wishes to see results soon. I do hope that you can meet our expectations. Don't disappoint us."

The call ended, and Winter stood up, looking down upon the tiny figures beneath her through her window.

"Foolish bastards. Do they really think that I would allow them to take away what's mine? This girl is merely a stepping stone for what I have planned. They can scheme away all they like, but it won't change the fact that I will get what I want in the end."

Winter turned around and changed the display on her monitor to show Snow in her new room, huddled in a fetal position in the corner.

She was so different from the last test subject that it was hard to imagine. However, Snow's personality would only make it easier for Winter to use her.

Winter was curious about what her contact had said to her. They knew where Snow had been hiding all this time. Why had they hidden Snow from her? They knew that she needed Snow for her experiments to continue. Why wait so long?

The answer was obvious. For the past fourteen years, since Snow was taken from her, the board had been trying to infiltrate her organization with people who worked solely for them. They must have succeeded in doing so. It seemed that she would need to make an example of them.

"Such fools, desperately clinging to make-believe power. None of them even realize that even without Snow, the experiments will continue. I never did say that she was the only one."

"You called, ma'am," the man who brought Snow to her said as he entered the room.

"Yes. Ensure that both testing rooms A and B are prepared. Make sure Snow is taken to testing room B."

"But, ma'am, that's the room that she—"

"It doesn't matter. All that matters is ensuring that after all this time, it still works."

"Of course, ma'am."

"Oh, and make sure that all members of the Intelligence department report to observation room B; we have a few rats that need to be disposed of."

"Ahh~!"

"Subject's vitals are rising. Should we continue?"

"Yes, increase power by twenty percent."

"But, ma'am, we have never gone over thirty percent This could damage the subject."

"It does not matter. They must understand what it means to defy me. Increase by twenty percent."

"Yes, ma'am."

"Ahh~!"

"Vitals are reaching critical levels. Ma'am, if we don't stop this, the subject will die."

"Fine, stop the machine. Record the data, and we can begin again tomorrow. I will make sure that she understands her place."

"Yes, ma'am."

Winter entered the room where the subject was being tested.

"You're pathetic. If you had just given up and listened to me, I could have had you become my successor. You just had to let the new test subject go. You can't blame anyone but yourself for your current state."

"N…"

"Huh? What was that?" she asked, leaning in closer.

"Sn-Snow… free…" the white-haired woman mumbled, too weak to talk.

"How adorable, you gave it a name. However, that right there was a mistake. I told you not to get attached to it, but you didn't listen to me."

"She is not an it…"

"Hmm. You still seem to have enough energy to talk. Let's go another round. Reboot the machine. She wants to continue!"

The video stopped playing just before the woman's screams echoed throughout the room again. Snow held her hand up to the screen, touching the woman as a tear rolled down her face.

"Why?"

"Hmm? What's that?" Winter asked her.

"Why? Why did you d-do that to her?"

"Because she disobeyed me and took you away from me. You were created to replace her, but she grew attached and tried to keep you from me. Instead, she just prolonged the inevitable.

"What happened to her?"

"That's something you don't need to worry about. For now, what you need to worry about is why you're here," she said, turning off the monitor.

"I hope that the day of rest we gave you is more than enough to help you calm down because today, you will undergo experiments just like the test subject that preceded you."

"No… I don't want to…"

Snow felt scared. She saw the pain that the white-haired woman endured during these so-called "experiments," and she wanted no part in them.

"Sorry, that's non-negotiable. Fortunately, the testing methods used back then have greatly changed since then. Keeping the test subject alive and healthy is preferable to not doing so. Now, let's stop wasting time and see if my theory bears fruit.

"Theory?"

Before Snow could properly ask her question, she was dragged away by two men in suits.

She desperately tried to break free, but they held still, forcing her back into the elevator. Any attempt to talk was met with silence to show her that nothing she tried would save her from her fate.

It wasn't long before she was dragged into a plain white room surrounded by observation windows near the ceiling. The only thing in the room was a stand holding a clear orb placed in the middle of the room.

"Place your hands on the orb," Winter said through the speakers.

She was currently on the other side of the glass, sitting in an observation room with board members who were more than eager to start this project after all this time.

Snow followed instructions, knowing that there was nothing else she could do. The moment her hands touched, the orb began to glow.

Little did Snow realize that the orb she touched was a polished crystal, similar to the one she had touched before at the university.

"That's it, don't let go," Winter told her over the speaker.

Snow was scared of the people watching her, but so far, just touching the orb wasn't causing her any pain. What did they do to make the white-haired woman scream so much?

"You see, just like the last test subject, this one is about to bring out the dormant energy of the crystal," Winter said, explaining to the board.

"Hmm. That may be so, but if I recall, the last one was able to generate far more energy than this one," one of the members said, observing the energy output from the crystal.

"Indeed, just looking at the results now is quite disappointing," said another.

"There is a reason for that, obviously," Winter said, showing them the screen. "Our new test subject is younger than the previous test subject, and this is the first time she's been hooked up to this machine. Due to some urgent concerns, there wasn't enough time to get her used to the draining process. We should be able to harvest more energy from her as time passes. Though she is the only test subject we have, we must be careful about what we do."

"Understandable," an older board member said, rising to his feet. "You have a week to get the draining sequence up to thirty percent. I know you won't make the same mistake as last time."

The board members didn't stay long, soon following the older man who had just left.

"Tsk. Greasy old man. Snow, you can stop now," Winter said over the speaker. "Follow your escort to Room R. A surprise awaits you there."

"Alright?" Snow said, confused by how brief this "experiment" was, but she didn't have time to think about that because she was soon led out of the room by several men, who guided her to where Room R was. Honestly, the room was quite nice, almost like a rec room for relaxing.

"Huh?" Snow stopped when she felt something soft brush against her leg. "Mochi?"

A bunny at her feet resembled Mochi closely, but it couldn't be Mochi. There was no way Mochi could be here. They were supposed to be with—

"Snow?"

Chapter 27

"Huh? Where am I?"

The last thing Snow remembered was Mochi and Faye arriving at the same facility where she was being held, and the next thing she knew, she found herself floating alone in a dark void. But for some reason, she didn't feel scared. She felt safe.

Wait, there was a light.

She felt her body slowly move toward the light. She felt scared to leave, but the moment she laid her eyes on the woman before her, she felt safe. It was the white-haired woman from before, holding Snow in her arms.

"Congratulations, ma'am, it's a healthy baby girl."

"Thank you, thank you, thank you," the woman said, embracing Snow. "Thank you, my precious Snow. Thank you for being here.

"Ugh, took you long enough. The doctors were about to give you an emergency C-section," Winter said, walking into the room. Much to Snow's surprise, she soon found that she couldn't talk. Winter looked much younger than before, but her eyes were the same.

"Give me the child's hand." Winter grabbed Snow's hand and placed a familiar crystal in it, eagerly watching as it glowed. "Finally! It's finally worked!

You've done well, my daughter. Soon, you will be free, and she will take your place."

"Finally, the nightmares can end," the woman said, gazing at Snow with longing. Only then did Snow realize why she felt such a strong connection to this woman. She was her mother.

The light surrounding her dimmed, and when she opened her eyes again, she found herself struggling to stand in the middle of a playroom.

"That's it, Snow. You are doing great; mommy believes in you," her mother said, smiling from across the room. Snow found herself drawn to her, waddling her way across the treacherous floor filled with toys toward her mother.

"You've done very well," her mother said, catching Snow before she fell. "Mommy is very proud."

"No, Mommy is disappointed," Winter said, standing in the corner of the room. "She's already one year old and just started walking. Her body is much weaker than originally thought."

"She is only a baby, mother. It takes time for them to grow, or do you not remember?"

"That hardly matters, Aurora. The longer it takes for your child to develop, the longer you remain the only viable test subject. Don't forget the reason why you had this thing. Her only purpose is to serve as your replacement."

"Yes, mother…"

The scene faded to black again, and this time, Snow opened her eyes to find herself in Winter's office.

"You can't be serious!" Winter yelled, startling Snow. "You're willing to throw away years of work because you're starting to grow a conscience? That test subject is the future of this company!"

"She's not a test subject! She's my daughter!" Aurora yelled back at her.

Ugh, this is why I told you over and over again never to get attached. She was born to free you and give you a life, but you're willing to throw that away because she's your daughter? I thought you were willing to do whatever it took to be free, even sacrifice the one you gave birth to.

"I was! But I…"

"Pathetic to think that you're my daughter. I'm going to give you this one last opportunity. Stop causing trouble and bring her to the testing room. She's three years old now. Her body should be able to handle a bit of pain. And just remember, I can take away your freedom just as easily as I gave it to you."

"Yes, mother…" Aurora replied in defeat, picking Snow up in her arms and walking out of the room.

"Don't worry, mommy will protect you… no matter the cost," she said as the scene faded to black before Snow opened her eyes to a familiar dream.

"Get her!"

"Don't let her get away!"

"How? How did this happen?" Aurora asked, holding Snow in her arms as she ran through the forest. "How?"

Snow was scared because she knew how this ended.

"Don't worry, sweetie, nothing bad is going to happen to us. It's alright," Aurora said as she made her way through the thickness of the trees to lose the men chasing them.

It took some time, but Aurora eventually managed to elude their pursuers for the time being, making her way to the pond from which Snow would eventually emerge.

"There we go, sweetie. See, nice and safe," Aurora said, placing Snow on the ground and caressing her cheek. "Sweetie. I need to go away for a while, and you need to stay here. Can you do that for me?"

Aurora looked nervously around, ensuring that there was no one nearby before bringing out a necklace and placing it around her neck.

"Good, I knew you could be a brave girl for me. Snow sweetie, I need you to take this and keep it with you always. Take this and never let it go. I need to take care of a few things before we can see each other again."

"Can I see you again?" Snow asked, finding the ability to talk once more.

"Yes, I promise we will see each other again," she said, kissing Snow on her forehead, causing Snow to cry for a reason she couldn't understand.

"There she is!" one of the men chasing them yelled out.

"Tsk, they found us faster than expected," Aurora said. The purple strands in her hair sparkled in the dim rays of the sun, distracting Snow from the horrors of what was happening.

"Don't worry, sweetie. I will return to you. I promise." Aurora stood up, prepared to leave, but Snow didn't want her to go. Snow sensed that something terrible would happen if she did.

"Don't go!" Snow managed to yell once again, but it was already too late.

Before Snow could understand what was happening, she felt her feet leave the ground. Aurora smiled at her, a look of longing on her face.

"Remember, I will always love you."

The water was cold on impact. Snow wanted nothing more than to swim out of the pond, but she was too small. She had to wait. She had to be patient. She had to wait until the time was right.

The water around her grew colder and colder, slowly freezing around her and forming a cocoon of ice. And that was the last thing she remembered before entering the dream.

"I… I remember everything!"

"Snow? Are you alright?" Faye asked, seeing Snow's eyes open.

"Faye? Faye, I remember everything. From the moment I was born to the moment I woke up in the pond. Everything is so clear now," she said, sitting up from Faye's lap.

"Snow, your stutter? It's gone."

"It is…"

Ever since Snow had woken up, she had been struggling with a stutter. It had improved since she made all of her friends, but it was still there. This was the first time she was able to speak without it hindering her words.

"Faye, how did you do that? How were you able to help me get my memories back?

When Snow first entered the room, she was shocked to see Faye and Mochi there. She had no idea why her grandmother would want them, but Faye promised to explain once she tried something. And that "something" was giving Snow back all of her forgotten memories.

"Snow, you need to understand that we are here for a reason," Faye said, trying to find the best way to tell Snow the truth.

"I know. They want me, or rather us, to power the crystal, right?"

"Yes, I know she isn't ready for this, but what else do you expect me to do?" Faye said, to Snow's confusion.

Mochi jumped up on the sofa they were sitting on, getting in between them. Snow wanted to pet him, but for some reason, she felt she shouldn't.

"I'm telling you that if we wait any longer, her life will be in danger. She has no idea how to control her output. If things go wrong, she…"

"Faye? Who are you talking to?" Snow asked, curious about what Faye was saying.

"No, I'm telling her, and you can't stop me," she said, picking up Mochi and placing him on the ground.

"Faye? What's going on?"

"Alright, this will sound crazy, but you need to listen. Magic is real."

"Huh? Faye, I don't think that this is the time for jokes," Snow said back to her, more concerned with why Faye was there than listening to jokes.

"It's not a joke. Here, look at this."

Faye lifted the right side of her hair, revealing an earring with the same crystal as Snow's necklace.

"That's… how did you get that?"

"It's a longer story than the one I'm telling you now, but all you need to know is that these crystals are connected to those with magic."

"Faye, are you sure you're alright?" Snow asked, worried the people here might have messed with her mind. "Do you need to lie down?"

"I'm perfectly fine," Faye replied, knowing that explaining this wasn't going to be easy. "Magic is real. Snow, you asked who I was just talking to. I was talking to Mochi."

"…I need to see if I can find you a wet towel or maybe a nurse."

This was insane. Faye wasn't making any sense to Snow, and her words were only making Snow worry more.

"No, she'll understand. I just need more time," Faye said, looking straight at Mochi.

"That's it. I'm calling for help!" Snow declared, rising to her feet. There was no way she could let this continue.

"Snow! Just wait!" Faye yelled, grabbing her hand. "Just think about it. How were you able to remain in that pond for fourteen years? I saw your memories. You used your magic to protect yourself in a cocoon of ice. You only emerged because it was time."

"My memories? How did you?"

Snow was confused. There was no way that magic could exist, but Faye was right. How else could she have survived all that time in the pond? Was she still missing memories? No, that was impossible. She remembered even her own birth. There could be no way she could have forgotten something else.

"Because of my magic," Faye said, holding Snow's hands as Mochi nuzzled against Snow's right leg. "Mochi says that it's okay to be scared. We're here for you."

"I… I think I need a minute."

She was overwhelmed. She didn't want to believe that something as crazy as magic was real, but she couldn't help but believe Faye's words. Too many strange things had already happened to her in a short period.

Faye helped her back to her seat, waiting for Snow to process everything.

"So, let me get this straight. You have magic."

"Yes."

"And you can talk to animals?"

"Basically, yes. My magic allows me to connect to another's mind. It allows me to talk to animals like you said, but it even allowed me to help you remember who you are."

"Thank you."

Snow didn't know what to say besides that. She had regained a part of herself that she didn't even realize was lost. It was a gift she could never repay, but at the same time, she felt like she had just entered somewhere she shouldn't have.

"Snow, they came for me not long after they took you. These people who are holding us here want us not just to power their stupid crystals, but they want our magic as well. Magic is a beautiful thing. It's something that allows the unimaginable to exist, but for that reason, it is very dangerous as well."

"What do you mean?"

"They want to turn our magic into a weapon."

Chapter 28

"What do you mean that you haven't found her yet!" Autumn yelled at the end of the phone. "My daughter has been missing for over a week now, and you aren't doing anything about it!"

"Ma'am, please, we don't have any evidence to go off of at the moment," the police officer replied. "The people who took your daughter somehow managed to do it without anyone properly seeing their faces. There is no security footage of them abducting her, not even a license plate for the vehicle they might have used to take her."

"You people are worthless! If you don't find my daughter, then I will!"

Autumn hung up the phone in a fit of rage and fell onto her couch. Snow had been missing for ten days, and there were still no clues about where she had been taken. Autumn spent day after day trying to figure out where she could have gone, but it was no use. Just as the cops said, there was no evidence.

"Mom, you have to eat," Lily said, walking into the room with a sandwich and a glass of water.

"I'm not hungry."

"Mom, please. You haven't eaten properly in days."

Lily was worried about her mother. She was a mess, and who could blame her? Lily almost passed out from shock when she heard what had happened to Snow.

"How can I eat when, for all we know, Snow could be starving right now… maybe even…"

"Mom, don't, just don't," Lily said, sitting down next to her mother. "Snow is strong. She'll be alright. I'm also worried about her, but she wouldn't want you running yourself into the ground searching for her."

"And what am I supposed to do?"

"You need to rest. I'll stay by the phone to make sure that—"

Lily was interrupted by the sound of the doorbell being rung.

"Huh? Who could—"

"Snow!"

Upon hearing the doorbell, Autumn jumped to her feet and rushed to the door. She desperately hoped it would be news about Snow, but to her dismay, no one was there. She looked around to ensure she didn't miss anything, only for her eyes to land on a large brown envelope on her doorstep.

"Mom, what is it? Is there any news about Snow?"

"I don't know," Lily said, picking up the envelope and finding a strand of frizzy black hair stuck to it.

"Let's see what's inside."

Lily led her mother back inside and took the envelope from her. When she opened it, she was shocked to see stacks of photographs inside.

"What the hell is this!"

Lily almost threw up seeing multiple photos of a woman with white hair and purple highlights being tortured. Strapped to various machines, being lit on fire, whipped, fingers broken, and others that Lily didn't want to think about.

Who would dare send them something this twisted? They even made the woman look like Snow. Lily had to get rid of these photos.

"Mom, don't look," she said, gathering the photos, knowing that her mother must be even more disturbed than she was. "Mom, please give me that."

"Aurora…"

"What did you say?" Lily asked, noticing that what was in her mother's hands was not a photo like the others but a detailed document featuring the photo of the woman from the other pictures.

"Here, read," Autumn said, showing her daughter the document.

I.C.E.

Date: 8/14/2009

Test Subject #1: Aurora Fall

Gender: F

Age: 25

Status: Unknown

Information: Test Subject #1 is the daughter of President Winter. She is to be used as a test subject to activate the strange energy stored in newly discovered crystals gifted by a mysterious benefactor. The subject often resisted but became more docile after giving birth through artificial insemination. The daughter was classified as Test Subject #2. After birth, the amount of energy harnessed from the subject has increased. The daughter was supposed to take place so that Test Subject #1 could inherit her mother's position.

Certain side effects have appeared on Test Subject #1 after giving birth. Spontaneous combustion, producing purple flames, and sudden loss of clarity have appeared. There is a possible connection to the crystal, but there is not enough evidence to prove it.

Test Subject #1 became too close with their replacement and escaped the facility with Test Subject #2.

Test Subject #1's escape attempt failed, but test Subject #2 is nowhere to be found. Test Subject #1 is being processed for further experimentation. Precautions will be made to prevent further escape.

New Classification: Test Subject Alpha.

Further Notes: The location of Test Subject #2 is unknown. Reclassified as Test Subject Beta. It must be found. All methods of interrogation on Test Subject Alpha have been authorized to be used.

"Mom, what is this? This woman, she looks almost identical to Snow. Is she?"

"She's Snow's biological mother!"

Chapter 29

"Estella, are you sure you want to do this?" Ember asked as they stood outside Autumn's home. Like everyone else, they were desperately searching for Snow.

During their search, Estella realized that her mother knew something about Snow that they didn't. She understood Adrienne wouldn't agree to take her out of worry, but she had no choice. She had to help Snow.

"I'll be fine," Estella said, ringing the doorbell.

"I'm sorry, but we don't want to… oh, it's you two," said Autumn, opening the door. "I'm sorry, there's still no news about Snow. You guys should—"

"We might have a clue about how to find her!"

"What did you say?" Autumn asked, slowly walking to the door. She was still shocked by what happened to Snow's birth mother, but she had to be strong.

"It's my mother," Estella said to them.

"She knows something about Snow. I think she can help.

"Please, you have to believe us."

Ember held Snow tightly. She didn't want to lose this chance to help her. They had to believe her.

"Get in the car."

Autumn didn't want to waste any more time than she already had. Back at court, she thought that Violet's warning was merely a threat.

It was foolish of her not to consider it until now. She wasted no time shoving all three girls into her car and making her way to Violet.

"Lily, it's probably best if you show the girls the document that came to us earlier," Autumn said to her daughter while driving. "Just don't show them any of the other pictures."

"Alright."

"Who is this? And why does she look like Snow?" Estella asked, looking at the document given to her.

"We believe that she is Snow's biological mother," Autumn replied.

"Here, let me… what? What the hell is this?" Ember exclaimed, staring at the document.

"Ember?"

"Why does this document have the same acronym as the people who volunteered to take care of my sister?"

"Do you mean your sister who fell into a coma after her unfortunate accident?" Autumn asked her.

"Yes. My mother found it hard to pay her hospital bills, and we were lucky when they came and offered to take care of her for free," she said with a pessimistic smile.

"At first, we were hesitant, but their facilities were amazing. My mother and I visit her once a week. Why would they have a document on Snow's biological mother?"

"I don't know, but we have to follow the lead we have. Estella, we need to go see your mother now."

"What a surprise. To think that you came all this way to see me," Violet said, cuffed to the table. "I would have dressed up, but as you can see, the only fashion here is orange jumpsuits."

"..."

"What? Nothing to say to your poor mother? The mother you betrayed? You even came here with the mother of the skank that did this to me."

"Call her a skank one more time, and I'll make sure that you'll never open your mouth again," Autumn said, unwilling to deal with this woman's bullshit. "My daughter is missing, and I think you know why."

"Do I? I don't recall ever wanting to take your daughter. I only wanted to get rid of her."

"Then explain this," Autumn said, placing the document about Aurora on the table.

"I was right!" she yelled, laughing hysterically.

"What's so funny?"

"What's funny is that I was right. That sk-daughter of yours is actually the daughter of my old cellmate."

"What?"

Autumn didn't understand. Did Violet know Aurora? How?

"Wow, you really don't know what you got yourself into, do you? I.C.E. or as it's better known, Infinite Customer Endorsement. They are a charity organization that helps those in need. However, that is just a front. Their true name is Inhuman Confinement & Experimentation. They kidnap certain individuals and experiment on them after having them touch a strange crystal. At least this was the case twenty years ago.

Aurora was my cellmate. She was the most prized test subject. Many test subjects perished over the years, but she always survived. I later learned this was because she was the President's daughter."

"Luckily for me, I wasn't there long. I was classified as what they call a "non-essential asset" and was released. They told me they would kill me if I told anyone about what happened there, but seeing how I'm in prison, there is little they can do to me now.

"I will tell it to you straight. If your daughter truly is Aurora's biological daughter, then there is no doubt in my mind that they have her. It would be best to give up on her. Your claim as a guardian is practically void against them, especially since she would now be with her grandmother."

"I refuse to believe that!" Autumn yelled, slamming her hands against the table and causing a scene.

"It would be better if you don't do that again," Violet said, giving her a warning as the guards loomed over them.

"It's fine, we're leaving."

Autumn had heard enough. She couldn't leave her daughter with these people. It was time for her to go on the counterattack and rescue her.

"Have a nice trip. Oh, and Estella, I hope you remember that girl fondly, just as she was. That place has a way of breaking people. I wish I could be there to see your faces when you met the broken and beaten girl that you once claimed to be your daughter!

Violet's repulsive laughter echoed through the room as they left. There was no longer any time to wait for the cops. They had to take action.

Chapter 30

"So I take it that you met with Faye," Winter said across the table to her granddaughter. "If I'm correct, you went to the same school together. Her bunny is very cute. To think that it followed her. Should I get you a pet as well?

"Why?"

"Hmm? Why what?" Winter asked, taking a bite of her salad.

She wanted to do something nice for her granddaughter and invite her to a proper dinner, but she refused to eat—such a bad child.

"Why is she here? I thought you wanted me because mom left you," Snow said, glaring at her.

"Oh, so you remember who test subject alpha is? How wonderful."

"She was my mother, your daughter… how? Why? Why did you do that to her?"

Snow couldn't understand it. Thanks to Faye, she was able to remember who she was, though this knowledge brought her even more pain. Her so-called "grandmother" tortured her daughter. Why?

"Progress requires sacrifice. I should know. My mother did similar things to me. It's how the world works. You need to show the world that you have power. That girl, Faye, and the other one we have are more or less insurance. We need them to ensure that progress continues even without you."

"Other one?"

Was there another person taken by her? How could she justify what she was doing?

"It's nothing that you need to concern yourself with. All you need to do is stay healthy and participate in every experiment we give you. If you do that, we can give you anything you desire: clothes, jewelry, books, an MS5. I know how much your generation loves playing video games. Though the internet will be cut."

"I want to go home," Snow told her, refusing to fall for any temptations offered to her. She just wanted to see Autumn and Lily again.

"My dear naïve granddaughter, this is your home. You may have managed to hide from me for the past fourteen years, but that doesn't mean you can act as if none of this is happening."

"You will stay here for the rest of my life, and after giving birth to a child of your own, they will take your place, and you will take mine. This cycle will always repeat itself. Trust me, in time, you will learn to accept this."

"No!" Snow yelled, slamming her hands against the table and spilling her untouched drink.

Tears started to form in her eyes, fearing that she would never see her friends or family again. She didn't want to meet the same fate as her birth mother.

"Believe what you want to... excuse me, I have a call to take. Make sure she doesn't do anything she'll regret," Winter said, receiving a call through her earbud.

A bodyguard stood silently behind Snow as Winter went to the next room to answer her call.

"What is it?" she asked, annoyed that she had been interrupted.

"Ma'am, we have a slight problem down here at the front desk."

"You called me because of that? Call security to take care of them."

"Ma'am, we can't. A woman and three teenage girls are here demanding that we give them back a girl called Snow. They said that they would call the cops if they didn't talk with you."

"Of course, they did," Winter replied in a dissatisfied tone. "I will be down there shortly."

Tsk, these must be the ones who took care of Snow. She knew she should have handled them. No matter; she could easily use them to break Snow's spirit.

"I'm sorry about that, but we have some uninvited guests that need my urgent attention," Winter said to Snow as she walked into the room.

"It's them!"

Snow didn't know why, but she sensed it had to be Autumn. She came for her.

"Don't get so happy just yet," she said, pressing a button on a remote to lower a TV from the ceiling.

The image displayed on the screen showed Autumn, Lily, Ember, and Estella. Each of them looked furious, though just seeing them put a smile on Snow's face as tears started to flow from her eyes.

"They will be leaving here without you. In fact, they will be more than willing to let you stay here, where you rightfully belong."

"You lie!" Snow yelled, attempting to throw her plate at her "grandmother," but the bodyguard stopped her.

"Believe what you will, but the truth is hard to deny. Stay here and watch the video. There is no audio, but I'm sure you'll understand the truth when you see those four walk out of here with smiles on their faces."

"No! I'm- ugh! Let go!"

The bodyguard held Snow in place, preventing her from following after Winter and keeping her from her family.

"Let me go to them!"

"Tsk, tsk, tsk. My poor, sweet granddaughter, do you really think they ever cared about you?" Winter said, caressing Snow's cheek. "Just look at where we are. They probably only came here to receive money for taking care of you."

"No, they love me!"

"Love? The mere notion of love is a lie. In this world, people only do things to benefit themselves and their egos. That woman only took you in to make herself look better. That girl whose mother was sent to jail used you to make it happen. None of them actually cared for you. But that doesn't matter to me because as long as you stay here with me, I will always find a use for you. Now, please be a good girl and enjoy the show."

"No! Stop! Let me go!"

Winter ignored Snow's pleas as she stepped into the elevator. It was time for her to meet the woman who had kindly taken care of her granddaughter.

"I said bring me my daughter!" Autumn yelled, furious that these people weren't listening to her.

She had come here asking if she could speak to the person in charge, but not only did they insult her, they claimed she was a bad mother for losing her daughter.

"Ma'am, your daughter isn't here," the man at the front desk said to her. "I called the president, and she says she will help you with your problem in any way she can, but you need to calm down. You are making a scene."

"You think that this is a scene? You better shut your mouth before I show you what it means to piss off a mother looking for her child."

"Ma'am, I—"

"I am sorry for making you wait," Winter said, appearing before the enraged woman.

"You… you look like Snow."

Autumn knew there was a connection between Snow and this woman the moment she saw her. The resemblance was uncanny.

"Perhaps it would be best if we had this discussion elsewhere."

"Fine," Autumn said, knowing she would have to at least humor this woman if she wanted Snow back.

"I'm glad you understand; please follow me."

Winter gave an evil grin as she led Autumn and the three girls to a private meeting room. This way, everything said would only be known by them and be seen by Snow.

"Allow me to introduce myself. I am Winter Fall, the president of I.C.E. What can I do for you?"

Winter calmly sat down, waiting for Autumn and the others to do the same, but they chose to stand.

"I want my daughter back."

"Your daughter? I'm sorry, ma'am, but I don't believe I can help with that."

"I want Snow back, and don't say you don't know her because this is more than enough proof of your shady activities."

Autumn pulled out the document about Aurora and placed it on the table.

"You know, if you had remained ignorant, I could have helped you adopt another child, but if you are so eager to force my hand, I will tell you the truth. Your daughter, or rather my granddaughter, is here, and she's watching you right now. She can see all of us, though not hear us. Now, if you would be so kind, sit down."

Autumn felt terrified. Snow was here, but she was out of her reach.

"What do you want with Snow?" Estella asked her, wondering how much of what her mother said was true.

"What every grandmother wants is to spend time with their grandchild."

"She's not your granddaughter! She's my sister! Give her back!"

Lily didn't care who this old hag was. She wanted her sister back and would do anything to get her back.

"You call her your granddaughter when you abused her mother, your daughter," Ember said, bringing up what she read in the document.

"Sigh, if I keep having to listen to these brats talk, we won't get anywhere."

Winter had no patience for ill-mannered brats like this, but she would tolerate it for now.

"That's enough, girls," Autumn said, taking control of the girls and sitting down as Winter instructed her. "I want my daughter back. You kidnapped her and took her away from her family against her will. I want her back, or I'm pressing charges."

"Charges? For what? All I did was bring my granddaughter back home. True, my methods were a bit on the rough side, but she is happy here. And Miss Ember, we have met before. Our company is helping your sister. There is a chance she may wake up soon. Though if you don't want to."

"Stop. Don't bring any more children into this than you already have." Autumn refused to allow more innocent girls to suffer. She would protect all of these girls. "I am Snow's legal guardian. Despite your claim to be her grandmother, what you did was kidnapping and imprisonment. You have no right to keep her here."

"Perhaps you're right, and perhaps that black and pink-haired girl with the rabbit would also be considered kidnapping."

"Wait! The reason that Faye has been missing was because of you!"

Ember couldn't believe it. Why were the people she cared about being put in danger?

"You have taken things too far!" Autumn yelled, unable to hold back her anger.

"And what are you going to do about it?" Winter arrogantly asked, snapping her fingers to have a briefcase brought to her.

"What is that?"

"This? This is your incentive."

Winter opened the briefcase to reveal a ton of money.

"What?"

"Right here is one hundred thousand dollars. Please take this money and leave. Never come back, forget about Snow, and live your life. Oh, and forget about the other girls as well."

"No, I refuse. I could never accept money and abandon my child and the innocent. I refuse to leave here without Snow."

"Oh, but you will, and you will do so with a smile."

Autumn yelled, "I would never do that!" refusing to yield to her.

"It's funny that you think you have a choice in this matter. All I need to do is give my bodyguard the signal, and he'll snap Snow's arm. And if you try to stop me, he'll break her legs. If you try to harm me, he'll break both her arms and legs. And if you refuse my deal, I will have him break her fingers, then toes, then ankles, then the wrist, then elbows, then kneecap, and then her shoulder blades. She'll be crippled for the rest of her life."

"You're a monster…"

"I'll kill you!" Lily yelled, ready to attack Winter, but Ember and Estella held her back.

"Very good. At least three of you realize the gravity of the situation. You claim to be her mother, but you are nothing more than a fool who gave her false hope. Even your appearance today will only make her suffer. How do you think she will react when she sees her precious family walk away after taking the money to abandon her? I'm sure you'll be quite devastated."

"You are a monster," Autumn said, holding back her tears.

"Say what you want, but we'll never see each other again, because if I see any of you four around here again, you know what will happen to her. Now come, take your money; you've earned it. Oh, and don't forget to smile."

"…"

Autumn could do nothing but say what she was told, taking the briefcase filled with dirty money while a smile was etched across her face. Inside, she was crying. She just wanted to help her child, but instead, she made things even worse.

"It's been a pleasure."

Chapter 31

"No, no, no!"

Snow couldn't believe what she was seeing. Autumn was taking the money her grandmother offered her. No, this had to be some sort of trick. She couldn't let Autumn leave. She had to go to her.

"Argh! You little bi—ugh!"

Before the bodyguard realized what had happened, Snow threw her glass of water in his face and then kicked him in his family jewels, sending him to his knees.

"Come on, come on, open!" she yelled, trying to open the elevator, but it could only be accessed by authorized personnel.

Seeing that there was no other way, Snow had to take the stairs.

She rushed to the emergency staircase, making her way down as fast as she could, but it wasn't long before the alarms went off. They knew she was trying to escape and would stop at nothing to prevent her from doing so.

"She's up there! On the nineteenth floor!"

"Move in to intercept! Don't use more force than necessary!"

"Don't let her escape!"

"No…"

Snow had to think. If they caught her, there wouldn't be another chance like this. She had to hide and slowly make her way out of there.

Storming onto the nineteenth floor was the best thing she could do at the moment, and luckily for her, there was no one around. She made her way to a random room, only to find herself in an archive.

Documents from past experiments filled the room. Snow wanted nothing more than to see if there was information about her birth mother here, but she needed to hide before it was too late.

Seeing a small space between a few boxes, she crawled between them and did her best to cover up any gaps. She needed to be quiet to avoid being found.

"Search every room! I want her found and brought to me!"

Snow covered her mouth silently, hearing the men trash the room searching for her. She was scared but needed to remain as silent as possible. She didn't want to get caught. If she could escape, she could return to Autumn and save Faye. All she had to do was stay quiet.

The men continued to search, tossing box after box aside in a hope of finding her, but luckily, they never did.

"Continue searching the other rooms. She is somewhere around here. Miss Fall will have our heads if we can't find her! Now go!"

The men left the room, allowing Snow to let out a sigh of relief. They were so close to discovering her that she almost had a heart attack.

Feeling it was safe, Snow slowly crawled out from her hiding place, only to see that there was still one man in the room facing away from her. She had to get back to her hiding spot before—

Just as Snow began to back up, she accidentally bumped into one of the boxes, causing a book on top of it to fall to the ground.

Out of fear, Snow quickly crawled back into her hiding spot, but it was evident he had heard her. She was doomed.

"Huh, what was that?" the man asked, looking around the room, only to discover Snow's hiding space. "Looks like my lucky day. I'm bound to get a promotion for bringing you back. Get over here!"

"No! Let me go!" Snow yelled, trying to break free of his grip around her arm, but it was useless.

"Come on, don't make this any more difficult than it-ack."

The man's eyes rolled back in his head as he fell face-first to the ground. Standing above him was the girl with frizzy black hair, wearing a lab coat.

"Thank heavens I—"

"No! Stay away!" Snow yelled at her, unsure if she could trust this girl, given that she had knocked the man out with the book in her hands.

"Shh~! Are you trying to get us caught?" the girl silently yelled, glancing quickly back at the door in anticipation of more men arriving.

"W-who are you?"

"That doesn't matter. I—"

"Are you working with them? Do you enjoy tearing me away from my family? Was this your plan all along?

"No, it's… it's not. I can't, um, please. It's hard for me to think right now. Please just come with me. I can help you."

The girl looked clearly nervous, and it didn't seem like she was working for her grandmother, but Snow wasn't sure. The last time she was with this girl, she was kidnapped. There was no way she could go along with this girl.

"Please. We don't have time. Uh… she's not going to like this. She told me to get you quickly, but should I?"

The girl started talking to herself, causing Snow to take a few steps back. This girl was already strange, but now she was talking to herself.

"Where is Bauer?" a man's voice called from outside the room. "Bauer, get your ass out here. We are searching the eighteenth floor next! Bauer!"

"Please! We have to go! It's not safe here!" the girl yelled, grabbing Snow's hands.

"No! I can't trust you!' Snow yelled, pushing her away. She wanted to go back to her family, but there was no way she could trust this girl. It was too risky. "Fine, she's going to get mad at me already," the girl said, making up her mind. "I was sent here by your mother!"

"My mother?"

So Autumn didn't abandon her. She still didn't know how much she could trust her, but if Autumn sent her, she had no choice but to pay attention.

"Yes. She sent me here to get you. No, come on! We have to hide," she said, pulling down a book on the bookshelf, revealing a hidden room.

Before Snow could consider whether to enter, the girl pushed her into the dark, concealed room, quickly following behind her.

"What are you—mph~!"

The girl covered Snow's mouth as the door to the secret room closed and the archive doors opened.

"Shh! We need to be extra quiet.

"Bauer, where are you? Bauer! All men return to floor nineteen. The girl has taken down Bauer; she could be dangerous. Permission to use tranquilizer darts is granted. I refuse to lose her like we lost her mother all those years ago."

The man looked around the room much more violently than last time, toppling every bookshelf he could and storming through the place before leaving.

"Who are you? How do you know my mother?" Snow asked as soon as the girl removed her hands from her mouth.

"There's no time. I need to concentrate," the girl replied, trying to avoid revealing more to Snow. It was too risky, and she wasn't ready. This was never part of the plan.

"Concentrate on what?" Snow asked, finally finding a light switch and turning on the lights. "Tell me what's going on?"

"I can't… I'm not allowed to. Please just let me concentrate," she said as a purple spark appeared before her.

"What do you mean that you're not allowed? Please tell me. What do you know? What's going on?"

"I c-can't!" the girl said, sounding as if there was a great strain on her body.

Within a matter of seconds, they started to connect to one another, forming a solid purple vortex.

"What is this?"

Snow couldn't help but be in awe of what she was seeing. After Faye told her about the existence of magic, she was still quite skeptical, but this… this finally made everything seem real.

"This is our way out of here," the girl said, looking exhausted. "I can't… I'm not allowed to say anything more than this. Please come with me."

"But the others?"

Faye and the other girl were still there. She was so concerned about escaping that she almost forgot about them. She couldn't leave them, not knowing what her grandmother had planned for them.

"The others? You are all that matters. We have to go. Your mother sent me to get you. The others don't matter."

"What?"

Autumn would never say that. Snow was right not to trust this girl fully. She used Autumn to try to trick her. This had to be some test from her grandmother. If she went with this girl, then she would be punished, and so would the others.

"Come on, we don't have time. They'll find this place soon. We need to go. Now."

"No."

Snow took a step back. This was twisted. Playing with her like this. How could Winter do this to her?

"What? We have to go; I can't keep this portal open for much longer. Please, I'm trying to take you back to where you belong. She needs you, and you need her."

"My mother wouldn't want me to leave others to suffer," Snow said firmly to her, learning well from the love and kindness that Autumn showered her with.

"Your moth-no, you have it wrong! That woman won't understand what you are. She'll fear you after learning the truth. They all do. Please, this is your chance to be free."

"Alright," Snow said, putting a smile on the girl's face, walking towards her.

"Thank you for listening. I promise tha—what?"

Before the girl could react, Snow pushed her inside the strange portal. A pained look was etched across her face as the portal vanished, leaving Snow alone once more.

She fell to her knees, unable to determine whether she made the right choice. Tears flowed from her eyes as the secret door opened behind her.

"You should have gone with her while you still had the chance to," Winter said, looking at the pathetic excuse for her granddaughter. She would have taken the chance, not wasted it, if she were in her position.

"My mother, what did you do to her?"

"I gave her the only option she had, and she took it. It's not my fault you didn't trust me when I told you. I can understand that you are stressed after seeing what happened, but that was by no means an excuse to try to escape. I'll have to make sure to increase security around here. You won't be able to attempt an escape again."

"But I didn't escape. I stayed. I passed your test, right?"

"Test? You thought that frizzy-haired girl was a test? No, no, no, she was here to help you. I don't know why she wanted to, and I don't care. You're still here, and you'll never leave."

"No…"

Snow felt defeated. This was her chance to escape, and she wasted it. She could have sought help from the outside, but she didn't.

"Take her back to the testing room. It's time that we show her how naughty girls are punished."

"Yes, ma'am," the men behind her said in unison, dragging a lifeless Snow away.

Chapter 32

-Several Hours Later-

"Don't get comfortable. We'll be back for you in the morning," the two guards said, tossing Snow on the ground.

For several hours, her grandmother kept her hooked to the machine, draining her energy. After a while, they would increase the intensity of the machine. It only stopped when it began to overload, electrocuting Snow in the process and temporarily paralyzing her body. It was only when this happened that Winter deemed it appropriate to give her a break.

"You monsters! What did you do to her?" Faye yelled, rushing to Snow's side.

She looked awful. It was almost as if her life force was being drained away. Faye had been warned that this would happen if she got caught, but she could never have expected it. Snow was that crazy old lady's granddaughter. To do something like this to her own flesh and blood was appalling.

"Quiet unless you wish to take her place."

"Take her place, I'll make—"

"It's fine, we're sorry," a girl in a wheelchair said, approaching them. Her black hair stood out in the stark white room, and the smile on her face seemed forced. She was none other than the third test subject, Terra; Ember's sister.

"Please continue to do a good job, and I promise we will behave in the future."

"Tsk. At least one of you knows your place," the men said, leaving the room.

"Terra, why did you do that?"

Faye couldn't understand Terra's reasoning for letting those men go after what they did to Snow.

"To get them away from her, of course," Terra said, dropping her kind and obedient act. She had been here longer than these two, and this was just one of the methods she used to stay out of trouble. "Come on, let's get her to her bed."

Faye knew that Terra was right. She should have been more concerned about Snow's safety than picking a fight. She lifted Snow with ease, carrying her to her bed. It was fortunate that they all slept in the same room. Otherwise, Snow would still be left alone on the ground right now.

Seconds after Faye laid Snow down on her bed, Mochi came over and began to nuzzle her cheek, slowly bringing her back to consciousness.

"Ugh. M-Mochi? What are—my body, why is it, owww?" Snow moaned out in pain.

"Snow, what happened to you?" Faye asked, worried for her.

"I... I tried to escape."

"What? Why would you try and do something so foolish?"

"She did something to my mother to make her leave me here."

Snow couldn't help but remember the forced smile etched across Autumn's face as she took the money Winter offered her.

"Your mother was here?" Terra asked, wondering what sick game Winter was playing at that time.

"She was, and so was Lily, Estella, and Ember."

"Ember was here?"

Tears began to well up in her eyes. It had been so long since she last saw Ember.

"Terra, could you please tell us how you ended up here?" Snow asked, seeking something to help distract her from the pain.

"Sigh, I guess you two deserve to know the truth," Terra replied, knowing she couldn't hide this from them forever.

"As you must know already, the last time Ember and I talked wasn't a pleasant experience for either of us. While Ember was venting her frustrations at me, she accidentally stepped out into the street, not noticing an oncoming car. I pulled her out of the way just in time but ended up getting hit myself."

"By the time I regained consciousness several days after the accident, I could no longer move or feel my legs. I had become paralyzed from the waist down. I was told that I would never be able to walk again."

"Wait, Ember said, you were in a coma. How were you awake?" Snow asked curiously.

"That was a lie told to her and our mother. It was a lie created by I.C.E. They paid off the doctors to tell my family that I would never wake up again. Every time they visited me, I was injected with a heavy narcotic. They even set it up so that the bills needed to take care of me were double what they would normally have been, all so they could trick my mother into signing over her rights so that I could be treated."

"Not to mention the worst thing of all. My accident was no accident. It was intentional. The car that hit me that day was owned by I.C.E. They were planning from the start to run over Ember, but I got in their way. Honestly, they didn't care who they hit as long as they got a test subject."

"Unlike you and Faye, I don't have magic. I was used to test what would happen when they redirected the energy siphoned from people like you back into—ack… my body."

"Terra! You're coughing up blood again!" Faye yelled, worried for her.

"It's alright; it's just a side effect of the tests, and it's no big deal. As you can see, my body isn't compatible with magic. No matter what they do, it won't work. The original energy that they tried to have me absorb belonged to your mother."

"Terra… I'm sorry," Snow said, feeling worse now than before.

Everyone she cared about was getting hurt because of her. Maybe it would have been better if she had stayed on the ice.

"There's no need to be sorry. You're not the one that did this to me. You have nothing to feel guilty about. I should be the one that is sorry because if you wanted to escape, you should have come to me first."

Chapter 33

"Perfect, just after two weeks of testing, and she's already able to handle this much," Winter said, reviewing the data from the most recent experiments.

Ever since that woman, Autumn, came here and Snow attempted to escape, things have been going quite well. Although there is currently no news about the girl who breached her security and tried to run off with Snow, their numbers have been up.

Unlike her unfortunate daughter, who could barely reach fifty percent, her beloved granddaughter had achieved sixty percent without any adverse side effects. There were no signs of her producing magic, making her the perfect battery and subject.

Yes, Winter had long been aware of the presence of magic. It was quite interesting, and she was more than willing to exploit it for her gain.

If they continued at the desired rate, they could get Snow up to seventy percent, maybe even eighty percent. As for Faye, she couldn't even reach forty percent before they had to stop. It wasn't a bad start, but they needed to obtain as many results as possible.

Strangely enough, when some of her scientists went behind her back and tested the bunny that came with Faye, they discovered they could achieve a five percent result. While this was not a large amount, the fact that it yielded results opened up a whole new realm of possibilities.

As for Terra, that girl has been a true test subject to observe the adverse effects of magic on those who are incompatible with it. However, her health declines daily, much like those who came before her. There were still many other girls she could pick up from the streets. She would need to ensure that her men brought her a complete specimen this time and not a cripple.

"Ma'am, the investors and the board are quite pleased with the initial results. They want to know when phase two can begin," Winter's secretary informed her with a bright smile.

"Tell them I'm glad they are pleased with the current results, but phase two is still not ready. The injection of magic into a non-compatible specimen causes cellular decay. We will continue testing our current test subject, using the energy gathered from our new subject."

There was no need for them to know about Faye. Just in case Snow perishes, Faye was the perfect backup.

"Yes, ma'am," her secretary replied before leaving the room.

Despite her title, she was nothing more than a spy for the investors and the board. There was no point in sharing everything with her, especially regarding her real plan.

"Bring Snow in for more testing, and bring Terra with her," Winter instructed through the intercom. "Let's see how they react."

"Terra, that's insane. It's impossible," Faye said to her. "Snow won't be able to do that.

For the past week, Terra has been trying to explain her plan for them to escape, but Faye has always insisted that it's impossible.

"Faye, I don't understand why you keep saying it's impossible," Terra responded. "I might not completely understand magic, but you have it, and so does Snow. If you show her how to use her magic, we could use it to escape."

"Yeah, that's a great plan if it wasn't for the fact that I don't know what magic Snow has, let alone teach her. I broke too many rules when I came here; teaching a fledgling without permission is too dangerous. Besides, Snow is in no condition to move."

"I want to go home. I want to go home," Snow said, staring off into nothing.

Test after test, torture after torture. Is this what her mother experienced for years? How could she hold onto her sense of self when she was treated as nothing more than a lab rat?

"Snow, snap out of it; the tests are over," Faye said, shaking Snow back to reality.

"Sorry, I… I was just trying to think of my happy place. It helps to distract me from the pain."

"Faye, this is the fourth time she's zoned out like this today. We need to get her out of here."

"Terra, I understand, but it's just too risky. If we wait, I'm sure that—"

"Please… please just tell me what I have to do," Snow said to her, wanting this to end. If she could end it, she could go home. Back to Autumn, back to Lily, back to Ember, Estella, and all of her other friends.

"Snow, if I mess this up, you can die," Faye said, scared for her. In the past, many had tried what Snow wanted her to do, and they all perished in a raging purple inferno.

"I want to leave. I want to go home, please," Snow said, tears rolling down her cheeks. The pain from the experiments was too much. She wanted it to end.

"…You too, Mochi?" Faye said, looking back at Mochi. "He says that if it's you, you should be able to handle it. I hope that he's right. Sit down next to me, and we'll begin."

Snow complied, allowing Faye to take her hands and filling her with magical energy. For the first time in a while, Snow felt warm. She could feel the fatigue she had built up over the past week slowly leaving her body.

The warmth slowly faded as a nice cold feeling started to emanate from her heart. It felt natural. It felt—

"Get up. It's time for more tests!" a guard yelled, storming into the warm room and forcibly yanking her to her feet, disrupting the process.

"Wait! No! You can't take her yet! It's too dangerous!" Faye yelled, grabbing the guard's leg to stop him from leaving, but he easily kicked her aside.

"Move aside. You're lucky. No tests for you today, but you're coming with us," a second guard said, grabbing the handles of Terra's wheelchair.

Faye could do nothing as they were taken away.

Chapter 34

"You idiot!"

"I give you one simple job, and you failed not once but twice!" a woman in the shadows yelled at the frizzy black-haired girl, who was prostrating herself.

"I'm sorry! I'm sorry! I didn't think that she would be so reluctant to go! I promise if you give me another chance, I won't fail you!" the frizzy black-haired girl yelled back, pleading for forgiveness.

She had returned without Snow, and that was inexcusable. She couldn't allow herself to fail again. Everything must be done the way that "she" deems it.

"Hah! Do you think someone as incompetent as you deserves a second chance? I ought to have someone more worthy do the task."

"Please! I promise that I won't fail you again! I promise I will do anything it takes to ensure I bring Snow here. She won't be able to say no. I promise, please."

She couldn't fail. If she did, she would be abandoned and completely alone. She had to succeed, even if she had to go to Snow when she was at her weakest.

"Fine. I will give you one last chance," the woman said, sounding tired. "If you fail this time, you had best be prepared for the consequences that await you."

"Of course! I promise that I will bring you what you desire!"

"Good. Now go prepare…"

"...Ember, are you listening?" Estella asked, snapping her back to reality in the empty pet welfare club.

After what happened at I.C.E. no one knew what to do. Autumn felt powerless to stop them, and they were just teenagers. There was no way they could make a difference.

"Huh? Sorry, I... I just... is this my fault?" Ember asked, on the verge of tears. "Snow, Terra, Faye, each one of them was connected to me. Were they targeted because of me?"

"Ember, there's no way that can be true. It's not your fault."

Estella understood what it meant to blame oneself out of guilt, but none of this was Ember's fault. All of this could be blamed on one horrible woman: Snow's grandmother. For whatever reason, she wanted Snow and the others and wasn't afraid to use threats and money to get what she desired.

"It is my fault! Terra wouldn't have gotten hurt if it weren't for me. Snow wouldn't have gone to school and made herself known to them if it weren't for me. And Faye… I'm a monster."

Ember couldn't hold back her tears as she thought about Faye and everything she did for her. She loved her more than anything in the world, and because of her, she became entangled in this, too. Why did the people she loved have to suffer?

"It's not! Don't say that!" Estella yelled, hugging her and refusing to let her friend blame herself over a few mere coincidences. They had to stay strong for Snow. There was no way they would let it end here. Snow was strong. She and the others just needed to hold on a bit longer.

"You two! Check this out!" Lily yelled, bursting into the room with the other girls not far behind her.

Each of them was informed about what happened to Snow, Terra, and Faye and were eager to help in the best way they knew how: Social Media.

"Thanks to everyone's efforts, the whole world knows that I.C.E. is involved in the disappearance of Snow. Even if they try to hide it, people will still lose trust in them, and they'll lose the power they have!"

"The police are launching a formal investigation into I.C.E. right now. They can claim they have no idea about Snow and Faye, but they can't cover up Terra. Ember, I promise we'll get the three of them back."

"Soon…" Soon, Estella could see Snow again, and then she could finally tell her how she felt. "Please stay safe…"

"Agh~!" Snow screamed in pain as they raised the absorption rate to seventy percent. She felt as though her body was being torn apart, and Terra wasn't much better.

Just as energy was drained from Snow, that same energy was being infused into Terra.

"Agh~!"

In the tests they had experienced before, they had never felt such pain. They wanted nothing more than for it to stop, but it wouldn't. Nor could they escape. They were firmly strapped to the machine, preventing any attempts at escape.

"Ma'am! These readings are breaking past our predicted results," one of the operators said to Winter. "Snow is producing higher amounts of energy than she did before."

"Perfect. Raise it up to eighty percent," Winter said, pleased by the results. Everything was going better than expected.

"Ma'am, the second subject is barely holding on as it is. Blood is leaking from her nose and eyes. If we don't stop now, she may die."

'Do you think I care? Raise it to eighty—no, raise it to ninety percent."

"Yes, ma'am. Raising the absorption rate to ninety percent.

"Agh~!"

Snow and Terra screamed even louder, feeling their bodies overwhelmed by the pain. Terra had lost consciousness from the agony, but Snow managed to stay awake. She felt a cold sensation starting to build up, gradually becoming unpleasant. That discomfort intensified, turning uncomfortable and eventually painful. It soon became unbearable to suppress, and then—

Chapter 35

"I'm here! Come on out!" Autumn yelled in the middle of an empty parking garage.

It was only a few hours earlier that she had received a knock on her front door. When she opened it, she found a small envelope containing instructions she needed to follow if she ever wanted to see Snow again.

"I knew you'd come," the frizzy black-haired girl said, stepping out of the shadows.

"You! You're the girl who was with Snow that night she was taken! You took her!"

Autumn grabbed the girl and shoved her against one of the cement columns, nearly causing the girl's head to hit the column.

"Why? Why did you take her? Give her back!"

All she wanted was for Snow to be safe. It was because of this girl and Winter that her daughter was suffering. They had to pay.

"I-I didn't take her!" the girl said nervously. "But I can show you the way to her."

"What are you talking about? I know that I.C.E. has her! The cops won't listen, social media has failed, there's nothing I can do!"

"I… I can bring you to her, but you won't like it," the girl said, causing Autumn to loosen her grip.

"What? What do you mean?" Autumn asked, unsure of her words.

"Snow is different from you; she doesn't belong with you. She belongs with people like her."

"What are you saying!" Autumn yelled, growing even more upset. "She is my daughter!"

"Can you really say that once you learn the truth? Will you not fear her? Run away from her? Can you love her no matter what?"

The girl was dead serious right now. There was no nervousness in her words. She could bring Autumn to Snow, but things had already been set in motion that could not be stopped. Snow's awakening was only the beginning.

"I will! No matter what happens, I will stay by her side and always love her!"

"Fine, if that is how you really feel, then there's no reason for me to stop you. I hope you don't go back on your promise. And you might want to be prepared."

"Prepared for what?"

As she spoke with Autumn, the girl had already begun to concentrate on her magic, causing purple sparks to appear around her. Within seconds, they started to connect to one another, forming a solid purple vortex.

"What is this?"

Autumn had never seen anything like this in her life. What was it?

"This is our way to Snow," the girl said, pulling out two lab coats.

"Who said that I wanted to go with you?" Autumn asked, skeptical about this girl's true purpose.

Not only was she the last person Snow was with when she was kidnapped, but she also knew where Snow had been this entire time and even where she currently was. She had waited all this time without telling her anything. There was no way she could trust this girl, not to mention the strange vortex. How was this supposed to get her to Snow?

"I'm the only one who can get you to her. Do you think that you can get out without me?"

She was right. Without her, Autumn might never see Snow again.

"…Fine, but don't try anything funny," Autumn said, making her way through the vortex. Soon, she would be with Snow again.

"Is everyone okay?"

"Careful, there are live wires everywhere."

"Someone get a fire extinguisher. We need to put this out."

"Ma'am! Are you alright? Your face! It's bleeding!"

"Get away from me! This… this is beautiful!" Winter yelled, grazing her hand over the giant spike made of ice that had almost taken her head off. "To think such power resides in someone so small. How lovely."

"Ma'am, please, we need to check for everyone's safety!"

"Status report."

"W-what? Ma'am, there are people injured and—"

"Did I stutter? I said the status report," Winter said, looking down at the unconscious bodies of Snow and Terra.

She had no idea what had happened between the last test and this one, but she was more than impressed by such destructive power. It would be a waste not to use it.

"Several people are dead, many injured. We have already sent people down to retrieve the girls. They will be brought back to their quarters. Testing room A is completely destroyed. We will begin testing the properties of this ice soon."

"Good. We can't let this surprising result go to waste. Oh, and have someone bring me the black-and-pink-haired girl and her bunny. I do believe that they have some of the answers we seek."

Winter was certainly impressed by this. The last time she felt this way was when her wayward daughter almost burned down this entire building. Things were only going to get more interesting from here.

"Ma'am, we brought her," one of her men said, dragging Faye into her office minutes later.

"Good, you may go now."

"But ma'am…"

"It's fine. She won't do anything as long as she wishes for her friend's safety," Winter said, ordering the man to leave once more.

"As you wish," he replied, leaving without another word.

"What do you want with me?"

Faye had no intention of playing nice with this woman, as her worst fears were realized when Snow and Terra were brought back to the room unconscious. She would not give this woman the satisfaction that she craved.

"Good, straight to the point. I like that kind of attitude. I'll make this quick and simple. You're going to tell me everything that you know. And by everything, I mean everything. All you know about me, Snow, magic, and the people you are so desperate to protect."

"Oh, that's right. I know a lot more than you think, and I can even piece together random strands of information and figure out that you are hiding something that is worth more than Snow, and I want it. Now, are we going to do this the easy way or the hard way?"

Chapter 36

Snow woke up in a cold sweat. Her body felt ice cold. She wanted to curl up into a ball but couldn't find the energy to move.

What had happened? Why was… no! She remembered now. How? How could she do something like that? How could she have caused such destruction?

"Snow? You're awake," Terra said, wheeling herself over to Snow.

She had managed to wake up not long after they were brought here and remembered everything. Her body was sore, but this was something she was used to. There was no point in worrying about her fate; she was just glad to know Snow was alright.

"Terra? Did I… did I really use magic?" Snow asked, not fully sure how she made the ice appear. She could feel that she was the one who created it, but it terrified her, knowing that she couldn't control it. If she wasn't careful, she… no, she couldn't think like that. Faye and Terra were counting on her to use this magic to escape.

"You did. Are you alright?"

"I should be asking you that. Where's Faye and Mochi?"

"They were gone by the time I woke up. It looks like your grandmother sent for her. She should be fine, hopefully," Terra said, not quite sure what Winter was truly after.

"Terra, you aren't hurt, are you?"

"I'm fine. I've been through worse if you can't tell," she said, trying to lighten the tense mood surrounding them.

"Don't say that; you matter too," Snow said, refusing to let Terra put herself down just to ease the tension. "I didn't mean to harm you. I'm sorry."

"Snow, you didn't hurt me. Your grandmother did. You are not responsible for her actions. And you don't have to be scared of your magic. I think that it's wonderful."

"Really?"

Snow wasn't sure about that. She could still remember her ice piercing through the walls of the testing room and the screams of the people who were most likely injured because of her. She knew that she shouldn't care if they got hurt or not because they were the ones who kidnapped her, but she didn't want to harm others.

"Terra, I'm scared. What if I hurt the people I care about because of this magic?"

"You won't. You're too kind for that. Now, lie back down and get some rest. You must be exhausted. I'll get you some soup."

"Wait, I can help. You need rest, too."

"Stubborn, just like Ember. Fine, if you insist. Maybe we can enjoy some with Faye when she gets back."

"I hope she is okay and that nothing bad happens to her," Snow said, worried about the worst.

"You can't be serious!" Winter yelled, laughing at what Faye had just told her. "Do you honestly think I would believe that ridiculous story?"

"You're the one who asked. All I did was answer. It's up to you whether you believe it or not," Faye said, holding Mochi in her arms.

"I don't believe you, so tell me something I will believe."

"You know that the truth is what you make it, right? I told you the exact truth about magic and Snow, but you don't believe me."

"Fine. Let's assume I believe you and that I'm willing to negotiate your freedom. All you would have to do is tell me where the others are."

"Others?"

"Don't act dumb. Where are the others like you and Snow? Just like all those years ago with Aurora; she knew there had to be more. Since she couldn't find them, Snow was created as a new source of magic."

"I'm sorry, but I have no idea what you're talking about," Faye said, feigning ignorance, but that wouldn't work on Winter.

"Don't act dumb. The room that you, the cripple, and my granddaughter were so graciously given is equipped with surveillance equipment. I heard everything, even when you helped Snow with her magic, leading to this lovely scene," Winter said, pressing a button on her desk, allowing her monitor to display the current state of testing room A.

"W-what? What is this?" Faye asked, stunned by the sheer destruction before her.

"This is a result of what you did. Isn't it wonderful? To think that someone so small has so much power stored inside her. Just imagine what could have been done if more people like Snow existed."

"There aren't."

"Oh, but I believe there are. In fact, you are more than enough proof. At first, I thought this was nothing more than a special trait found in Aurora when she was a child, which was passed down to her daughter. But when my men found you, things changed. You are proof that there are more people with magic, not to mention the purple flames. Quite interesting, if I say so myself. But moving past that, all I want is the location of those who hold magic."

"So you can kidnap more people."

"Kidnap is such a crude word. I prefer acquiring more assets for my experiments."

"You are insane; however, given who you are, that makes sense."

"Call me what you like. It matters little to me. All that matters is that you tell me where the others are."

"I'm not going to do that, no matter what."

"Are you sure? That friend of yours, Terra. You have no idea what is happening to her, do you?"

"If you harm her—"

"It's already too late for that," Winter said, smiling at Faye's anger. "Our experiments with you and Snow are nothing more than drawing energy from you, energy you can regain over time. What we do to that crippled friend of yours is the exact opposite."

"We shove that energy into her body, hoping it can take hold. Unfortunately for her, her body isn't compatible with magic. The more we try to push it inside her, the greater her body resists, but at a cost. The magical energy is causing her cells to decay. Bit by bit, she is slowly dying. If we stop now, there's a chance that she can live until her forties, but if we continue, she won't last a week."

"You're a monster," Faye said, disturbed by Winter's words. "But you forgot one thing."

"And what was that?

Chapter 37

"Who exactly are you?" Autumn asked the young girl with frizzy black hair as they stepped through the portal, finding themselves in what seemed like an archive of some sort. Unbeknownst to Autumn, this was the same archive the girl had tried to escape with Snow.

"Who I am doesn't matter to you, now does it?" the girl responded, searching the room for the documents she needed to show Autumn.

"I think it does matter. You're just a child. You're no older than Snow. You appeared right before she disappeared and… and that thing we just went through. What the hell was that?"

"I told you before. It would help us get close to Snow."

"But where is she?"

Autumn knew she couldn't trust this girl, but she realized that this girl had information about Snow that she didn't. For now, she would have to rely on this girl to help Snow.

"Going directly to Snow is too dangerous. We have to be careful. I can't fail again. I have to succeed."

"Fail again? What do you mean?"

"Sigh. Seeing that it will take me a few minutes to find what I need to show you, I'll talk. Have you ever been saved by someone?"

"…No, that's right, you've only saved others. You don't understand what it means to have nothing. You don't understand what true pain is. Countless years of nothing but pain, only to be saved right before the brink."

"Just like Snow, I was saved and will do what I have to pay back that debt. Snow understands that."

"What? I would never…"

"You trained her to be your daughter when she already had a mother. A mother who cared and loved her. You took away the love meant for her."

"You have no idea what you're talking about. I didn't train Snow to be my daughter! I love her!"

"Of course you do. They all say that, and in the end, is that true?"

The girl understood the truth. Autumn's love was fake. It wasn't real. There was no way she could ever love Snow, just as deep down she… no, that didn't matter. All that mattered was taking Snow back.

"How dare you! I love Snow!"

Autumn was furious. How could this girl dare question her love for Snow?

"Would you say the same thing if you knew what she was?" the girl asked, handing Autumn the recent documents on Snow.

"What is this?"

Snow Fall
Age: seventeen
Gender: Female
Classification: Weapon

......

"What is this? This has to be some kind of sick joke!" Autumn yelled, reading the document. "Snow is not a weapon!"

"Say what you want, but soon you'll realize the truth. Snow never was yours. She's always existed for a higher purpose."

"I refuse to believe this! Now take me to Snow!"

Autumn was done messing around. She thought this girl was another poor soul like Snow, but she was nothing more than a monster.

"Take you to Snow? I can't do that. It's your job to find Snow. I have other things to do," she said, pulling out a golden locket. Upon opening it, Autumn saw a strange purple flame inside.

"What are you doing?"

"I'm sorry, but I don't have time to dilly-dally. So I need to ensure you find her as fast as possible."

Without warning, the girl dropped the flame into a stack of documents, setting them ablaze.

"All information about Snow needs to be disposed of. I do hope you find her because it will be your last time seeing her."

"Wait! Where are you going?" Autumn yelled, watching as the girl ran out of the room, leaving her behind with the growing fire.

Luckily, the sprinklers soon went off, but even after some time passed, the fire would not go out. It was only a matter of time before this whole building would be engulfed in flames.

Scared and confused, Autumn ran out of the room, trying to see where that girl had gone, but she couldn't find her no matter what. No, finding that girl didn't matter. She had to find Snow before it was too late.

Chapter 38

"It's me. Everything is going according to plan," a shadowy figure said through a communication device. "The girl will be brought to you. …Yes, I will make sure that she is completely abandoned. She will have no choice but to come back to you. It's only a matter of time now."

"Wow. This is amazing," Snow said, creating a small mound of ice on the ground before her.

She was still quite weak from before, but she felt increasingly curious about her magic. Despite the destruction she had caused with it earlier, she couldn't help but admire its beauty.

"Even though I'm seeing you do it, it feels unreal," Terra said, touching the ice and feeling the cold against her fingertips. "How are you doing this?"

"I don't know," Snow said, concentrating a bit more as she formed a snowman out of ice. "It just feels natural. I have to put an image in my mind, and I can create it. I don't know how to describe this feeling. It's almost as if this has always been a part of me."

"I almost wish I could use magic too," Terra said, even more intrigued by her abilities. "Though I think you should take it easy for now. Eat more of your soup; you need the energy."

"You sound like a mother."

"Well, always taking care of Ember taught me a thing or two."

"Hmm, I wonder if… it worked. Would you like some ice soup?" Snow said, trying to joke around. It was the best way for her to forget about what she had done.

"Come on, stop playing around. That bowl was for Faye," Terra said, unable to hold back her smile.

"It's fine. I'm not that hungry for soup. I don't think I have the stomach to eat anything right now," Faye said, entering the room with Mochi.

Snow was glad to see that she was unharmed and safe. The same could be said for Mochi, who was so excited to see her that he ran over and jumped on her lap.

"Faye, we were so worried!"

"Worried? You don't know how nervous I was when they took you and Terra away. Not to mention when they came here, dragging me away to your grandmother, who told me what happened. I almost passed out from shock."

"Please tell me that neither of you is hurt?"

"We're fine, just a little bruised up," Terra said, relieved to see that Faye was alright as well. "But look at what Snow can do now."

"She did this? Did she freeze the soup? That's amazing!" Faye yelled, happy to see that everything turned out all right.

She had been scared that this would all end up in flames, just like those who had tried before. The stories she heard still frightened her, and she was half-expecting to ignite in flames or be frozen solid right here and now.

"Thanks, but to be honest, I'm a bit scared of it," Snow admitted to her. She was having fun with her magic but knew how dangerous it was.

"There is nothing to be scared of," Faye said, coming over and grabbing Snow's cold hands. "This is your magic. There's no reason to fear using it. Trust me, in time, this feeling of fear will go away. I can say that from experience, especially since I use a mental type of magic. It was scary for me at first too."

"Thanks. I don't know what I would do without you, Faye."

Snow embraced Faye, knowing that she could maintain her sanity because of her, Terra, and Mochi.

"Faye, what did they want from you?" Terra asked, curious about why they had let Faye walk back into the room instead of being escorted.

"Well, it's just as you probably expected. Right after they brought you two in, they took me out. They wanted to know about your magic. They, or rather your grandmother, wanted me to tell her the location of people like us. People who could use magic."

"I didn't tell her anything, but she won't give up. I tried to convince her that she wouldn't dare harm us, knowing that she needed us, but I don't think she cares anymore. She will increase the tests from here, and Terra, you…"

"I know," Terra said, not wanting to say it out loud. "I've known for a while."

"Then that's more than enough reason for us to escape. We have to escape, and to be honest, this looks like our best chance. Thanks to what Snow did, there must have been a lot of people fixing the testing area she was in. Using her magic, we can get past most of the security systems.

"Faye, Snow is in no condition to move. She needs rest. We should wait to ensure we are safe before we decide to do anything."

"Terra, we don't have the time for that. You don't have the time for that. We need to get you to a hospital."

"But—"

"Faye's right," Snow said, rising to her feet. "We need to get out of here."

She felt a bit lightheaded, but she could move. Snow was trying to hide it, but she could tell that she was in pain, and the longer they stayed here, the more pain she would experience. They needed to listen to Faye and escape.

"See, Snow agrees with me. Please, Terra. I don't want to lose you again."

"Sigh, fine, but we have to be safe about this. And if we're about to be caught, leave me."

"But—"

"No buts. This is the only way I will agree to this rash plan."

Terra was determined to keep these two safe, no matter the cost.

"Fine!" Faye yelled, struggling to agree with Terra.

"Alright, but if that happens, we will come back for you," Snow said, determined to reunite Ember with her sister.

"Okay, now that we have that settled, it's time—"

Faye's words were interrupted as several loud alarms went off.

"That's the fire alarm! The building is on fire!" Snow yelled, panicking a bit. "What are we going to do now?"

"We have to seize this opportunity to escape. If we get outside, your grandmother won't be able to stop us. We can all get away!" Faye yelled, grabbing the handles of Terra's wheelchair and pushing her toward the door. "Come on, Snow, we have to go!"

"Alright!" Snow yelled, running toward the still-locked door.

"You need to freeze the door's controls; doing so will cause it to open."

Snow wasn't sure what to do, so she could only listen to Faye, who seemed to know what she was doing. If she didn't do this, there was no telling if anyone would come for them afterward.

"Okay, here goes."

Snow placed her hands against the door's control panel, concentrating on it, freezing it bit by bit until a small spark came from it, almost hitting her. A click sounded as the door automatically opened because of its failsafe.

"Good job! Now let's go!" Faye yelled, pushing Terra out of the room first, with Snow quickly following after them.

"I don't think we can take the elevator in the event of a fire, so we must make our way down the emergency exit. It's the"

"Snow?"

"What?"

Snow stopped dead in her tracks, hearing a voice she had only recently remembered: her mother's.

"Snow? What are you doing? Come on! We have to go!" Terra yelled, confused about why Snow had halted all of a sudden.

"Don't worry, sweetie, mommy loves you. Granny is just a sour puss."

"Mom?"

Without thinking, Snow began to follow her mother's voice as if in a trance. It wasn't long before she reached another locked door. Using the same trick she had used to break out of their room, she opened the door.

"What are you doing? We need to… go?"

Faye stopped, noticing the contents of the room. It was a bedroom that appeared to have been unused for years, but one thing stood out: a singular framed photo.

"Snow, we shouldn't be here. We don't have time," Faye said, trying to convince her to leave, but Snow was drawn toward the picture.

"Mom…"

Picking up the framed photo, Snow saw an image of a woman holding a baby who looked just like her. That woman was her mother, and the baby was her.

Why? Why couldn't she have grown up with her mother? Why did they have to suffer? They could have lived together as a family if it weren't for her grandmother. She could have gone to school, made friends, and fallen in love.

She could only live her life recently, but now it was clear to her just how much she missed. Fourteen years stuck in that ice, lost in a stupid dream where she thought she was abandoned by the world.

"I know that it must be hard, but we can't stay here. We need to go before it's too late. We need… huh?"

"We need to give her a minute," Terra said, tugging at Faye's shirt. They couldn't get in her way now. Snow needed this time to come to terms with everything. She needed time alone.

"But we don't… fine, but please hurry," Faye said, taking Terra and Mochi out of the room with her, leaving Snow alone to say her goodbyes.

"Mom, I'm sorry. If it wasn't for me, you could have been free. You could have had a life. You could have done so many things if you had just sacrificed me. Because of me, you're gone. I'm sorry."

Snow couldn't stop herself from crying, holding the framed picture against her chest.

"It's a mother's job to care for their children. You have nothing to be sorry for."

"What?"

The frizzy-black-haired girl emerged from the shadows with a nervous expression on her face.

"You! Why are you here? Is this another trick from my grandmother? Get away from me!"

"Wait! I swear that I'm not an ally of your grandmother! I could never work for someone like her. She is a monster. I'm sorry about what happened before and the time before that. I only wanted to help."

The girl looked sincere, but it was hard for Snow to believe her words.

"What do you want? This place is on fire. You should run while you can," Snow said, rising to her feet and placing the framed picture back where it came from.

"I can't, not without you," the girl said, looking desperately at her. "I can't leave you here. You need to live."

"Why are you so insistent about helping me?" Snow yelled, getting frustrated with this girl. "Is it my magic? Is that what you want? I never asked for this stupid power! It stole my life away from me! I lost years of my life because of this stupid magic! My friends suffered from it. My family suffers because of it! And most importantly, my mother suffered from it!"

"I don't care about magic! All I want is a normal life where I can be happy!"

"I swear, you'll be happy if you come with me!" the girl yelled, holding her hand. "You may not want your magic, but you can't change the fact that you have it. You don't belong with these people. I can bring you someplace where you can be safe."

"Safe? Did that safety apply to my mother? No one came to her aid, and now she is gone!"

"Gone? She isn't gone."

Chapter 39

"What are you talking about?" Snow asked, confused by what she had just heard.

"Your mother is alive," the girl said, pausing once more, almost as if debating whether to tell her.

"She's alive?"

No, this couldn't be true. There was no way that her mother could still be alive?

"Yes, she is, but I shouldn't be telling you this. She didn't want you to know."

"Didn't want me to know?"

Didn't her mother abandon her? Is that why she never came back for her?"

"I wasn't supposed to tell you. She wanted to tell you everything herself, but some things keep her from doing so. I can bring you to your mother, but you must trust me."

"Trust you? I don't even know you. How can I tell if anything you say is true? You have magic like Faye and me, but that only gives me more reasons to be cautious of you."

"Faye?"

"Yes, the girl with the pink and black hair. For someone who says they are here to help me, you don't know about the people dragged into this mess."

"Yes, I can't prove anything, but you have to believe me. I'm only here to help take you back to where you belong. You need to come with me."

"No, I won't leave my friends behind. They are too important to me."

"You really don't get it, do you?" the girl asked, her weak tone turning dark. "Those people aren't your friends. That family you made here doesn't matter. They are just obstacles trying to get in the way of your true home. Your true family."

"True family? They are my true family! They took me in and cared for me! Who do you think you are to say that to me?" Snow yelled, furious that this girl would dare talk about the ones she loved as if they were nothing.

The air became cold, and Snow wanted nothing more than to attack this girl, but she couldn't. She had to get back to the people who needed her.

"Stop! If you go now, there will be no turning back! If you want to keep your so-called family and friends safe, you need to come with me!"

The girl sounded desperate, but Snow didn't care.

"You dare threaten my family!"

Snow couldn't stop herself. Before she knew it, an icicle was pressed right up against the girl's throat.

"I'm not trying to threaten you at all," the girl said, slowly backing away from the ice, her tone calming. "I'm trying to warn you that if you don't come with me, more harm will come. If you leave, no one else will be harmed."

"I'll protect them."

"It's too early for you to think you can solve all your problems with magic. You can barely control it. Please come with me. They will all turn their backs on you. None of them will choose to stay by your side."

"For the last time, no…"

"Snow! What's going on in there?" Faye yelled from the other side of the door. "Are you alright? I'm coming in!"

"Don't say I didn't warn you." The girl said back to Snow with a saddened look.

"Snow! Why were you yelling?" Faye asked, storming into the room.

"That's because…" When Snow turned around, the girl was gone. "Sorry, it was nothing. Come on, let's get going."

"Sure," Faye said, glancing back at the spot Snow had been looking at one last time before following her out of the room.

"What the hell do you mean that they escaped?" Winter yelled, throwing the vase on her desk at the nearest wall, shattering it into pieces.

"Ma'am, I'm sorry, but by the time we got to their room, they were gone," her aide said, sweating profusely. "I promise we will do everything we can to find them."

"You'd better because you know better than anyone what it means to fail me."

"Yes, ma'am!"

Winter gripped her head, wondering what the hell was going on. One second, she was interrogating that Faye girl, and the next, she was getting a report of a fire on the nineteenth floor. What the hell was happening?

"And what of the fire? Why is the alarm still going off?"

"Ma'am, the fire refuses to go out. The purple flames won't be extinguished by water or fire extinguishers. The fire has already started to engulf a few floors. There is still time for us to evacuate, but it's only a matter of time before those outside notice this. If they find the girls, they…"

"Tsk, find the girls! Find them now!"

"M-Ma'am?"

"You dense fool, find them! I don't care how many people it takes. They need to be found!" Winter yelled, dismissing the man. "Damn, that ungrateful girl is finally making her move."

"What is it now? I'm not in the mood," she said, answering her intercom.

"Ma'am, we have an intruder on the twenty-fourth floor. She's attacking those who come close to her. Should we use lethal force?"

"An intruder? What the hell are you talking about?" Winter opened her surveillance monitors for the twenty-fourth floor and was quite pleased with what she saw. "Bring her to me."

"Ma'am?"

"I swear I must work with deaf people. Bring the woman to me unharmed."

"Yes, ma'am!

Finally, at least one thing was going in her way. Who cared if the building was burning down? She could always rebuild. And so what if Snow was trying to escape? So long as she held onto what Snow cared about most, there was no way that she would ever leave.

"Thank you, Autumn, you've made things so much easier."

Chapter 40

"Alan, what the hell are you doing? We have an order to find the girls and evacuate," one of the guards said to another, trying to get him to move.

"I know that, Greg, but look," he said, pointing in front of him.

"Is that a bunny?"

"Yeah, don't you remember? One of the girls had this bunny. I think it was the one with pink and black hair. If the bunny is here, that means that she might be close by."

"That has to be the most idiotic thing you've ever said to me. It's just a cute bunny. If you want it so much, just grab it. I don't want to die in this inferno."

"See, I knew you would think it was cute. Now stay still, you little bunny."

"I think we can say the same to you," Faye said, stepping out from the nearest corner.

"See! I told you! Who's the idiot now?"

"Still you! Grab her!"

"Sorry, but no can do," Faye said, watching as both men stopped moving just out of her reach.

"What? What the hell is this?" Greg yelled, looking down to see that his feet were frozen to the ground.

"Good job, Snow. I told you that you just needed a little practice," Terra told her as Snow wheeled her out from the same corner that Faye had hidden behind.

"She did perfect," Faye said, agreeing with her as she grabbed the keys from Greg's belt.

"Give those back!"

"Sorry, but we're going to need these to escape. Oh yes, this one has a fob. The other three didn't."

"Other three? Wait, no, that's not the point! Free us! We're here to get you out of here! The building is burning down! We could all die if we stay here for too long!"

"That's the point," Faye said to them. "We know you're here to help us, but that's only so you can bring us back to Winter. We refuse to be captured again. We're freeing ourselves."

"Are you stupid! Even with those keys, there's no way that you'll escape from her!" Alan yelled.

"That is something we have to find out. Come on, girls!" Faye yelled, taking a much more influential role in leading them than Snow had initially thought possible.

"Wait! You can leave us here!"

"Don't worry, the ice isn't that thick!" Snow yelled back to them as they started to walk up the stairs. "You should be able to break out after a few minutes!"

That would give them enough time to escape. The fire was spreading quickly, and she had to hope that her choices were the right ones.

"Come on, Snow! Let's go!"

Faye led them to the stairs, and they slowly carried Terra down. Currently, they were on the tenth floor and slowly making their way down. They knew they needed to work fast, but ensuring they all escaped was Snow's main priority.

They took a slight detour with those guards to steal a car so they could escape. There was no way they could get away on foot, and luckily, Faye had her license. They just needed to reach the parking garage as quickly as possible.

"Thanks," Snow said to Faye, who went back up a flight of stairs to retrieve Terra's wheelchair.

They needed to make sure to have it with them just in case they were discovered, or Terra might get them all caught.

"For what?" Faye asked, as she picked up Terra again with Snow.

"For being here, both of you. If I were alone, I would have broken by now. My... mother must have been strong enough to survive what they did to her for all those years. I... no, it's nothing."

"Snow, you are stronger than you realize," Terra said, trying to comfort her. "You would have survived. I did, and I don't even have magic."

"Simply having magic won't help you survive something like this," Faye said to her. "You need something worth protecting. For you, it was Ember, and for Snow's mother, it was Snow herself."

"I guess you're right, but it is unfortunate that magic can't solve everything."

"I wish magic could solve everything. It's... well, it's not perfect."

"Faye, I know you didn't want to talk about it before, but since we have some time, could you tell me about where you're from, about others with magic?"

Snow was curious. Most of her life was still a mystery, even with her memories. She had spent fourteen years in a cocoon of ice. There was still so much more she wanted to know.

"Overall, it's nice. The people are friendly, and there's nothing to complain about. Besides having magic, everyone is the same."

"Then why did you leave? If you stayed there, you would have never ended up in this mess."

"I... I wanted a change."

Faye's words felt heavy to Snow. What had happened to her before they met?

"It's fine; there's no need to worry. That's all in the past now. It was ever since I met all of you."

"Do you not miss your family?" Terra asked.

"I do, but I'd rather not talk about it. Come on, we still have a lot more ground to cover. Those guards could come after us at any moment.

Chapter 41

"Ma'am, we've brought her," one of Winter's men said, shoving Autumn into her office.

"Let me go!" Autumn yelled at the man, trying to attack him, but unlike the others, he wasn't so easy to take down.

"You may go, Jacob. Make sure that those girls are found and evacuated from the building post haste. I will be down soon. Oh, and do whatever you want with the media. Those pesky flies should never have come here," Winter said, watching as news reporters and the fire department arrived at the base of the building.

"Yes, ma'am!" Jacob said, leaving without a second word.

"Where's Snow?" Autumn yelled, hoping to use this chance to attack her and force her to tell her where Snow was, but she stopped dead in her tracks, seeing the gun in Winter's hand.

"You know, you either have to be the dumbest or bravest person that I have ever met," Winter said, pointing her gun directly at Autumn. "I gave you a simple way out, yet here you are. Was the money not enough?"

"Shut up! I don't want your dirty money! I want my daughter back!"

"You are an idiot. To think that I would even consider you to be brave. That thing isn't your daughter. She's just an object for study. And by using her, I can achieve so many things."

"How dare you call her that! She's just an innocent girl! She didn't need to suffer all these years! What right do you have to treat her like this!"

Autumn was furious. How could someone who claims to be Snow's grandmother call her a thing and treat her as nothing more than a test subject? She was a monster.

"Really? I can tell by the look on your face that you just thought of me as a monster. So what? Snow was created for the sole purpose of taking her mother's place. This has always been her destiny. And if I'm a monster for trying to change the world, then so be it."

"Change the world?"

Autumn had no idea what this crazy woman was talking about. Why did she need Snow to change the world?

"Hmm, I guess I'll indulge you for now," Winter said in a conceited tone. "Snow is a battery. A source of energy, if you will. One that will power not only our world but also people."

"What?"

"Ugh, it's hard dealing with idiots, especially idiots who have been living with that thing for as long as they have. That girl Snow has magic."

"Magic, stop playing games with me!" Autumn yelled, refusing to believe that all of this was because some crazy old lady wanted magic.

"Games? Do you really think that everything you see here is a game? My building is burning, you managed to get in through a method that I do not know of, and those three girls have escaped."

"Snow's not here?"

What was all this for, then? Autumn was furious with herself! How could she have made Snow wait so long that she decided to escape?

"Of course, she's not here. Those girls escaped the moment the fire alarm went off. She used her magic to escape."

"Stop messing with me!" Autumn yelled, pissed off that Winter wouldn't take her seriously.

"And this is why I hate the young," Winter said, calmly walking toward Autumn and placing the gun against her head. "You don't listen. Though, honestly, I don't care if you believe me or not."

Autumn didn't know what to do. The cold barrel of the gun froze her in place. She expected that Winter wouldn't give up so easily, but to think she would threaten to kill her.

"Nothing to say now? Good. You see, I am in a bit of a bind with that girl escaping. She'll be caught, and I'll make sure that she never escapes again. To be honest, it's my fault all of this is happening. I allowed her too much freedom. I'll make sure that she is properly secured this time."

"You're a monster."

"Me a monster… well, I guess you have a point. I did give birth to that thing's mother. But does it look like I care? We live in a world where we are constantly growing. There is no time to wait. I will not let my name be forgotten to time. I have sacrificed too much to stop now."

"That's your justification? To be remembered? You're insane! Snow is just a kind, innocent girl, not a lab rat! You need to stop this! You need to let her go!" Autumn yelled, desperately begging for this woman to allow Snow to leave.

"Stop this? No, I think not," she said, turning her back to Autumn and walking to her desk.

Autumn knew she had a chance to attack her, but it was too risky. In the end, she just stood still from fear.

"Do you see this?" she asked, holding up a piece of ice in her free hand. "This was created by that thing you love so much. It's been several hours since she made it, and it's barely even melting in the palm of my hand."

"Power, magic, this ice, so many things about her kind are still a mystery to me, but I want to know them all. And I will. I don't care how long it takes. I will find others like her, and they will be used as test subjects too."

"But they are people! You can't do that!"

"Hmm, you really don't seem to get it. I can. I can do whatever I want. Here, come with me. There is something that I'm sure you'll enjoy seeing before we make our way to your beloved Snow."

"What is this?" Autumn asked as she was led into a monitoring room connected to Winter's office.

"Oh, this? Well, this is simply proof to show you that the thing you care about so much is nothing more than a dangerous monster," Winter said, playing the recordings.

"Agh~!"

The screen lit up, and Autumn saw something she wished she had not seen. Snow and a girl she did not know, strapped to a machine, screaming in pain.

"What are you doing to them!" Autumn yelled at Winter, furious that they would dare do this to her daughter and another innocent person.

"Oh, you misunderstand. This has already been done," Winter said back to her. We've done this time and time again with her since the time she's been in our possession. You see, this is all she's good for."

"You!"

If not for the gun threatening her life, she would have attacked Winter by now. But what mattered most was finding Snow, and she could not do that if she was shot.

"Go ahead and call me what you like, but it doesn't change what's about to happen next. You see, during this test, we decided to increase the absorption rate to ninety percent. Watch; it's about to happen."

"Agh~!"

Winter smiled as the next thing to appear on the stream was a giant, ice-cold icicle stabbing the camera, causing the screen to go dark.

"What was that?"

Autumn didn't want to believe what she had just seen. There was no way that someone as sweet as Snow was capable of doing something so destructive.

"It's exactly as you saw. In that split moment, her magic erupted from her body, destroying our lab and almost killing her in the process, as well as our other test subjects. I think you might know her better as the sister of the girl you were with last time. Unfortunately, she is a failure compared to everything else we are doing here. We're trying to make it so that regular people can use such magic, but even after all our tests always seem to do is slowly destroy her body."

"What?"

"Oh yes, I almost forgot you didn't know. Magic is quite harmful to those who do not possess it. And that is both true externally and internally. Mixing someone's DNA with magic will ultimately cause them to slowly begin to die. The more you pump it into their body, the faster their body decays. It truly is an almost marvelous thing. If we can find a way to weaponize it, then there are many different ways for us to profit from it."

"They're children! How could you do this to them? How could you treat them as nothing more than disposable pawns!"

Autumn bit her lip in frustration, causing a small trickle of blood to run down her chin.

"If you have to ask, you truly have not been listening to anything I've been saying, nor have you been paying attention to what happened. This right here is proof that the girl you call your daughter is nothing more than a monster who, surprisingly enough, gained a conscience. She may act intelligent but is nothing more than a product."

"People like you don't understand what it means to love someone else."

"I'm sorry?"

"Snow and even your daughter, you did these things to them without any remorse. How can you live with yourself knowing that you've harmed your own family like this?"

"Easy, I don't consider any of the people. When you get to where I am, you can't afford the luxury of seeing everyone as a person. However, you would not understand this. And speaking of my daughter, she's been through far worse than this. Here, let's take a trip down memory lane," Winter said, pressing another button, revealing a video of a woman who looked just like Snow."

"Agh~!"

"Come on, Aurora, this is only test two hundred and sixteen. We still have thirty-four tests before you even allow it to break. We can bring in your daughter if you don't want to continue. She's a year old now. I'm sure she's old enough to begin testing," Winter said through the recording.

"N-no… I'll continue, just don't… don't hurt her."

"Tsk! And here I am, trying to help you. All you need to realize is that she's not a real person. She's just a thing created to take your place. Don't you want this pain and suffering to end? All you to do is agree, and it will happen."

"N-never…"

"Fine, have it your way then."

"Agh~!"

After that, clips of the woman being tortured and experimented on flashed across the screen over and over again. She went through cruel and unusual punishment, and each time, she was given the same option, but she refused to take it. After a while, the video changed, and Winter was in it now, standing above a bloody and beaten Aurora.

"You stupid girl. I gave you the opportunity to tell me where she was. No matter how much interrogation we give you, she won't tell us where she is, will you?"

"Never… she's my daughter."

"No, she's the reason you're going to die here. Take her away and make sure that she doesn't escape this time. I don't care if you have to cut off her arms and legs to do it. We will find that child, and she'll enjoy a seat right next to yours."

"You monster! I swear one day I will kill you!"

Before the video ended, the woman was dragged off. This was the last recording ever made of her.

"You see, it doesn't matter if she was my daughter or not. She betrayed me and allowed my asset to escape. I don't care what I have to do or who I have to go through; I will get what I want in the end. And this time, you're lucky enough to help me. Come along. It's time we end this little rebellious streak of my granddaughter, don't you think?"

Chapter 42

"Ma'am, all files have been destroyed," the frizzy black-haired girl said, speaking into her phone.

"And Snow? Is she with you?" the woman asked from her phone.

"No. She still refused to come with me, even after I told her the truth."

"That's most unfortunate, but I expected you to fail, so I already sent her in to finish the job."

"Ma'am, please, her methods are too cruel. We don't even know if it will work," she said, not wanting to involve that person.

"She's never failed me before. Not like you have. Remember your place and finish the job. You will be punished for your failure when you return."

"But ma'am, I—"

The call was ended before she could express any more of her grievances.

"No… no, no, no! I can't be punished! Not again! I did everything I could to bring her back peacefully! Why do I have to be punished because she refused? I warned her over and over again. Ugh, why did she have to resort to using her? Or did she plan to use her from the start?"

"No, I'm mumbling to myself again; if she finds out, I'll be punished even worse," the girl said, realizing she was talking to no one. "I need to keep moving. I have to destroy all the files and data about them. Once they're gone, I can finally go get Snow. I just hope that I'm not too late."

She opened another portal, walked through it, and ended up inside Winter's office.

"Come on, move it already," Winter said, coming out of an adjacent room and pointing a gun at Autumn's back.

Winter's sudden appearance made her duck down quickly behind Winters's desk.

"While I doubt the fire will get this high, we have an appointment with your beloved daughter. She's going to be so happy to see you."

"You're crazy to think that I am willing to make Snow go back to you in exchange for my safety," Autumn said, neither realizing that the girl was there, listening to everything.

"Still, you understand nothing even after everything you just saw. Snow will give in regardless of what you say. That is, unless she wants to see you die. Love is a weakness. I do hope that you understand that at the very least."

"You only say that because you have no idea what it means to feel love. Someone like you would never understand what it means to love another person. Maybe you would not have done such terrible things if you did."

"Say all that you want. Your words can't hurt me. Now, get into the elevator. It's the only way we'll be there waiting for them."

She watched as Winter shoved Autumn into the elevator, making their way down to the first floor.

"That was close. I need to hurry," she said to herself as she made her way to the room where Winter and Autumn had just left.

While she felt sorry for Autumn, she had her orders, which mattered most right now.

"Not here, not here… where is it?" she asked herself, searching the room.

In addition to bringing back Snow and destroying all files on them, she needed to find a certain document. Finding it at this time was not easy, especially since it felt like searching for a needle in a haystack. She had already searched everywhere else. She had to find it. If she didn't, she—

"Do you not miss your family?" a voice asked from the monitor's speakers. It seemed that while she was looking for the document, she had accidentally turned on the monitor's sound.

She looked up at the screen, watching two girls carry another girl down the emergency stairs. One of those girls was none other than Snow, and it looked like they were nearing the fifth floor. Though on another monitor, she could see several men making their way to the emergency stairs, each eagerly pursuing the girls.

"Shit! They're going to be caught. I have to do something, but the document," she didn't want to leave the document she was looking for, but she couldn't let Snow get captured.

The room was starting to feel hotter. It was only a matter of time before the fire reached this floor and destroyed everything.

Winter was a fool to doubt the power of the flames she unleashed. However, at the same time, she regretted it, knowing what she had to do.

Opening a portal, she stepped through, appearing right before one of the men. Before anyone could properly react to what was happening, she opened a portal behind him and shoved him through it to the back alley behind the building. She had to hurry; if she missed any one of these, they could harm Snow, and her safety would be questioned.

"What the hell, who are you!" one of the men yelled, seeing what had happened to one of his allies.

She didn't bother to respond. She quickly opened the portal behind him, trying to knock him in, but, like the other one, he was not caught by surprise, so instead, she had to go for a more drastic option.

"Stay where you are or—ack! M-mommy…" The man's voice turned high-pitched as she kicked him in his family jewels, using this moment to push him straight into the portal.

"Snow, we're running out of time!" one of the girls below yelled, noticing the ruckus above. "We have to get out of here now!"

"Don't let them get away!" a guard yelled quickly, storming his way down the stairs, but she would not let him have his way. She opened the portal straight behind him and kicked him in the back of his knee, causing him to tumble down the stairs. She had to hurry because everything depended on these small moments that she was granting Snow.

Chapter 43

"Lily, where are we going?" Ember asked as she and Estella got into Lily's father's car. She was supposed to get it after she got her license, but there was no time to waste now.

"Weren't either of you paying attention!" Lily yelled, quickly driving out of the driveway. "That building I.C.E. is on fire! Snow's in there! I don't know where mom is right now, and she isn't picking up her phone, so we have to go without her."

"Wait, do you mean?"

"Yes! This is our chance to get Snow back! The media is reporting the strange fire all across the news now. There's no way that they won't want information about a kidnapping case when confronted live. We have to do this."

"Strange fire?" Estella asked, not understanding what Lily was saying.

"We're the same age, but it's like you girls don't even look at your phone when news pops up. Ugh, it doesn't matter; just go online and look it up."

"Alright, it can't be that strange…"

Ember couldn't believe what she was seeing. All across the news, the I.C.E. building was engulfed in purple flames.

"You can't be serious. This has to be a trick," Estella says, looking at the phone. "Magicians use certain minerals to change the color of fire. It has to be the same concept. No, wait, it couldn't. There's no way that something like that is possible. What am I even thinking?"

"It doesn't matter why the color of the fire is purple. All that matters is getting Snow and the others out of there."

"And how do you expect us to do that?" Ember asks, worried for Terra. She was helpless last time. How could she save her sister this time?

"There's no way that I'll be able to get the car close to the building. I'll need to find a place to park. All you two need to do is get the reporters to listen. Even if the cops are on their side, as long as the people believe us, there is a chance."

"And what about you? Aren't you going to help us?"

"No."

"What do you mean no?" Estella shouted, confused as to why Lily wouldn't help them free her sister.

"While you guys talk with the media, I'm going in. If there is still a chance that Snow is inside the building, I can't leave her there."

"Are you insane!" Ember yelled. "You can't go into a burning building!"

"WHAT CHOICE DO I HAVE!" Lily yelled at the top of her lungs, losing her cool demeanor. "For all we know, Snow and the others could be in there now, suffocating! I won't let her die! I already lost my father! I don't want to lose my sister!"

Tears rolled down Lily's cheeks. She hadn't felt this powerless since her father died. She knew it was foolish, but what choice did she have? She had to save Snow.

"Then we'll go with you. My sister is in there as well, not to mention Faye. They all need us."

"Agreed. It's better if we go together," Estella said, knowing that they would be more effective united, even if it was still risky.

"No, we can't go together. I have to go alone. I can't risk anyone else's life on this."

"But we're willing to do it for Snow and the others!"

"No, you're not! I'll do this! Trust me, please!"

"But Lily, we can—"

"No! We're here. Hurry and get over there now!" Lily yelled, stopping the car and seeing that a crowd of people had already started gathering several blocks away.

"Lily, please be safe," Ember said, knowing it was pointless to try to stop her, but that didn't mean she would let her go alone.

"But Ember, we can't leave her to do this alone."

"It will be alright."

Ember took Estella's hand and pulled her out of the car, both watching as Lily drove off.

"Ember, there is no way that we can let her go alone."

"I don't plan on it," Ember said, grabbing her hand and leading her towards the burning building. "In fact, we're going to be the ones doing this without her!"

"What are you talking about?"

"My sister is in there, Faye is in there, and Snow is in there. Those are people I care about. I don't wanna abandon them, not now, not ever. It'll take her some time to find a place to park her car. We need to get into the building before her."

"What? How do you expect us to do that?"

"Last time we were here, I saw an emergency exit beside the dumpsters. We will enter through there!" Ember yelled quickly, running through the streets and pulling Estella along with her. They had to get there before Lily.

She knew it was best to go to the media and tell them about all this, but there was no way she could let another person risk their life for the people she cared about, especially since one of them was her sibling. It had to be her.

"Ugh! Fine, let's do this!" Estella yelled, hardening her resolve, knowing that whatever happened next, it would affect both of them.

After several minutes of running, they finally managed to avoid the large crowd and made their way into the back alley. Luckily, the firefighters were trying to extinguish the fire from the front of the building, not the side. However, there was barely enough room for them to get in there.

The heat of the flames could be felt from outside, yet for some reason, it wasn't spreading toward other buildings nor diminishing under the weight of the water being pumped onto it.

Once they reached the door, Estella and Ember hesitated for a moment, gazing at it, wondering if Snow and the others were still on the other side. For all they knew, Snow and the others might have already been taken to another place. But they didn't know, and for that reason alone, they had to take this step. Hopefully, they could finally rescue the ones they loved.

Chapter 44

"Finally, only a few floors left to go," Faye said, realizing they had reached the fifth floor, but she knew they were already out of time. She could hear multiple doors on the floors above them opening. The guards would soon be upon them.

"Is there something wrong, Faye?" Snow asked, sounding concerned.

She was getting tired and worried they wouldn't be able to escape at this rate. The staircase already felt like a melting pot. The fire was spreading faster and faster. Carrying Terra was becoming exhausting, but there was no way they could leave her behind. Snow had to bring her back to Ember, no matter the cost.

"I'm fine. I thought I heard—"

"Ack! M-mommy!"

Suddenly, they heard a man cry out in pain. Looking up, they saw that all the guards Snow had frozen were now free.

"Snow, we're running out of time!" Faye yelled, knowing they had to move quickly. "We have to get out of here now!"

"Don't let them get away!" a guard yelled at them, quickly rushing down the stairs. While Snow's back was turned, trying to carry Terra, Faye saw a quick streak of black hair before that same guard began tumbling down the stairs.

"What's happening?" Terra yelled, unable to see what was going on in her current position.

"Someone seems to be distracting the guards. We need to go!" Faye yelled, realizing this was their chance.

"What? There's no way we can leave them after this. We need to help them."

"Terra, we can't. We can't do anything for them except get out of their way and continue our escape!"

"Snow, you agree, right?"

"Y-yeah," Snow said, pausing for a second, feeling a bit strange. The heat must be getting to her. It was getting harder for her to think straight.

"Snow, what are you talking about? We need to help them!" Terra yelled, confused by why Snow agreed to leave the person helping them.

"Terra, we need to go. There's no time to waste!" Faye yelled, sounding irritated. "Whoever they are, they're on our side. If we don't take advantage of the chance they're giving us, we're denying their efforts!"

"Ugh! Fine, you're right!"

Terra didn't want to admit it, but in her current state, there was nothing she could do. Unlike Snow and Faye, who had magic, she felt like nothing but a burden.

"Come on, Snow, stop spacing out and let's get moving!"

"Y-yeah, let's go," Snow said, realizing she was wasting time. She had to trust that Faye knew how to get them out. With her and Mochi around, she knew they would be safe. Wait… where's Mochi?

"I sent Mochi ahead of us to make sure that there was no one waiting for us downstairs," Faye said calmly without even batting an eye.

"Faye, this may not be the time or place to say this, but thank you. Thank you for being here. I don't know what would have happened to either of us without you," Snow said as they approached the third floor.

"Don't talk like that right now. The moment you do, bad things happen. We can't jinx ourselves now," Faye said with a smile. Soon, everything would be over, and they would leave this building and never return.

"Faye, how come I've never seen this side of you before?" Terra asked. She had known Faye for years, yet she had never seen Faye act like this until recently.

"What do you mean?"

"I mean, you're more confident than before. It's almost as if you're a different person."

"Terra, please, I've always been like this; I've just been a bit shy. We don't have time to talk about this pointless nonsense right now. We need to focus on what's important: our escape. Every second we waste talking is another second they get closer to us, and the person holding them back loses. We can talk about this later.

"Y-yeah… you're right," Terra said, agreeing with her.

"…"

Snow didn't say anything, but she noticed something strange about how Faye was speaking. What

Terra said made sense, though maybe she was overthinking it at the moment.

"Stop…"

Faye suddenly spoke, causing Snow to stop in her tracks.

"What are you doing?" Terra asked, looking confused for a second. "We're only on the second floor. We need to hurry. We're almost there. We have to escape now!"

"But you told us to stop?"

Snow is confused as to why Faye is acting as if she didn't say something.

"Sorry, I wasn't thinking straight. I'm trying to tell myself to stop thinking about pointless details. It must have slipped out. Come on, we have to hurry, please!"

"Hurry, they're almost at the ground floor!" one of the guards yelled, revealing to the three of them that the person helping them had failed.

"Come on, we need to move now!"

The three girls began hustling down the stairs toward the first floor, making their way to the emergency exit door.

Snow banged against the door, trying to open it, but it refused to budge. Someone had activated the electrical lock, leaving them trapped inside.

"What are we going to do now we're trapped?"

"We have to go out the front way!" Faye yelled, pointing to another door that led to the first floor of the building. Mochi was waiting for them, but something about this whole scenario felt wrong to Snow.

"Come on, we have to hurry. They're coming!"

"Don't let them escape!"
"Snow, please!"
"Fine, let's go!

Chapter 45

"Ember, we need to hurry. There isn't much time!" Estella yelled as they rushed into the building.

The heat of the flames felt even more intense than it did outside. If they stayed here too long, they would suffocate.

"Right!" Ember said, pulling out her phone. "I'll head upstairs to see if I can find them. You stay down here, just in case. We can't afford to miss them!"

"I understand! Let's—"

"My, my, it looks like two more rats scurried in when I wasn't looking," Winter said, leading Autumn out of the elevator and pressing her gun against Autumn's back.

"What are you doing? Let her go!" Ember yelled.

"Let her go? Then what bargaining chip will I have to make sure that girl stays here?"

"Girls, get out of here. I promise that everything will—ngh!"

"Everything will not be alright," Winter said, pressing the barrel of her gun deeper into Autumn's spine. "None of you will be leaving this place. Each one of you is going to be used to show Snow what happens when she tries to run."

"Wait? You mean that Snow is still in the building?" Estella asked, wanting to see Snow more than anything right now.

"Of course she is. She should be exiting that emergency staircase very soon. How funny is it that you came from the opposite side of the building? The two of you just have rotten luck. However, if you remain still and do what I say, I will reward the two of you. I'm certain that you are here for your sister?"

"What have you done to her!" Ember yelled, furious that the old hag would harm her family.

"Hmm, now that is a question. No, the real question is what I haven't done to her," Winter said, mocking Ember. "Your sister was a very valuable test subject. Despite being a useless cripple, she is more than resilient. Most subjects would have been long dead by now. Though that by no means is she going to live.

"Her fate has been determined from the moment we acquired her. I'd say she may have a few months to live at the most and that's if we stop using her as our precious lab rat."

"…What?"

Ember was stunned. There was no way this woman could be telling her the truth. Her sister was dying, and it was all her fault. No, that wasn't true. It couldn't be.

"You monster! How can you call yourself a human?" Estella yelled, standing up for Ember.

"Human? Do you really think being human is about being kind? The nature of all humans is to benefit their self-interest. That's all that matters—making it so we can gain more power, praise, or satisfy our ego. You are nothing more than children, but you'll see soon enough that life is not a fairy tale."

"You're wrong! There are people who are truly kind! Autumn and Snow help people because of their kindness!"

"If that's how they wish to live, then that only proves that they are weak. Look at where she is now. She came here, searching for a thing that she thinks to be her daughter, only to be taken hostage as a result. Her so-called kindness in an attempt to free her is going to get her precious daughter caught again. How ironic."

"I won't let you take Snow!" Autumn yelled.

"Really? Face it, you've all failed. Even if you do escape, I'm her biological relative. There's no way that you could hold onto her for long."

"You hag!" Ember yelled, letting her anger take over. "I'll—"

With a decisive blow, Ember was shot in the back of her right knee, collapsing onto the ground.

"EMBER!" Estella screamed, panicking as she watched her friend fall.

"Are you alright, ma'am?" Jacob asked, walking past the bleeding Ember.

"Of course, there was no need for you to interfere in the first place, but I guess she should feel happy about this. Now she can be a cripple just like her precious sister."

"Ember! Ember, hold on!" Estella yelled, rushing over to her and quickly tearing her shirt to apply pressure to Ember's wound.

"Agh~!"

Ember screamed out in pain while Estella did her best to stop the bleeding.

"You monster! She wasn't a threat! How could you shoot a child?" Autumn yelled, tears rolling down her face.

"If she didn't want to be shot, then she shouldn't have moved. She has no one to blame but herself," Winter said, a smug expression etched across her face.

"You're a monster!"

"We've been through this pointless conversation before. You can scream and complain all you want, but it won't change anything. And besides, even if I did care, it's too late to stop this. This building is on fire, and that thing is needed for me to continue my work. I will continue, no matter the cost."

"Ember, you have to stay awake! Look at me! Just look at me!" Estella yelled, trying to keep her friend conscious. She managed to slow down the bleeding a bit by using Ember's shirt as a tourniquet, but there was only so much she could do. Ember had already lost a lot of blood, and she feared what would happen if Ember passed out.

"Calm down; there's no way she would die from that," Winter said, brushing off Ember's pain as if it were nothing. "Her sister survived far worse."

"D-don't you talk about her!" Ember yelled, starting to feel dizzy from the loss of blood. She knew that if she passed out, the dizziness and pain would stop, but if she did, she would just become a hindrance to everyone else.

"See, what did I say? She's fine. But more importantly, I believe we should get ready to greet our guests. Their little rabbit is already here. I'm certain that they will be here soon," Winter said, noticing Mochi sitting next to the other emergency star door.

Everything was finally coming together. Snow would be hers, and this time, there would be no more options for escape.

Chapter 46

"Come on! We should be safe if we make it out through the front!" Faye yelled as the three of them emerged from the emergency stair doors. "All we need to do is… no…"

"Why hello there," Winter said with an evil grin. "It's a pleasure to see all of you here. Look, we have guests."

"Snow!"

Autumn was both scared and overjoyed to see that Snow was alright. She looked a little worse for wear, but she was safe, and that was all that mattered to her.

"Mom!" Snow yelled, overjoyed to see that Autumn was here for her, but that joy soon turned to fear the moment she saw the gun pointed at her back and Ember bleeding out on the floor.

"Oh, how lovely, a family reunion. If I cared, I would cry for the two of you. But I don't. I don't have any more time to deal with the lot of you. Come along, Snow, it's time we leave this place."

Winter looked confident that she would get her way, but Snow wasn't going to give in. She had magic now. She could save her friends and her mother. She didn't have to be afraid anymore.

"No! I refuse! I'll never go anywhere with you! I'm going home!" she shouted as they set Terra down on the ground.

"Home? Are you serious? This place was your home. Do you genuinely believe there's any place in this world where you belong? You exist for my benefit. Can't you see that resisting me causes more harm to others?"

"Shut up! I'm not your possession! I'm Snow Dust! The daughter of Autumn Dust, and I have the right to be free!" Snow shouted, rejecting the notion that her grandmother—no, this woman—could define her identity.

"Stop playing these foolish games. You know the truth. You know your purpose. And by the way, your mother is my daughter Aurora. Stop pretending that this pathetic woman is your mother. It's beneath you."

"Snow, you have to run! I'll be fine! Just take Faye and Terra and go!" Autumn yelled, knowing she had to be brave for Snow. If she faltered, Snow would suffer.

"Shut up, you annoying woman! You're not going anywhere," Winter said, pressing her gun deeper into Autumn's spine. "None of you are going anywhere without my say-so."

"Mom!"

"Enough of this nonsense! This woman is not your mother! Your mother is my daughter, Aurora Fall. That is who you are. Stop trying to pretend to be someone you're not!"

"Let them go!" Snow yelled, her anger rising.

How dare this woman threaten the people she loved? If she used her magic, she could get rid of Winter and save them.

"Snow, calm down," Terra told her, feeling the air grow colder around them.

"No, you don't have to be calm," Faye said, standing side by side with her. "You have every right to be upset. You have every right to want to protect those you love. You have to unleash your power."

"Faye, stop! We can't be rash here!" Terra yelled. "We have to—"

"Terra?" Across from them, Ember started to cry, seeing her sister awake after all this time. "Terra, I'm sorry. I'm sorry, but I didn't mean for this to happen. I'm—"

The echoing sound of a gunshot filled the room from Jacob's gun, silencing everyone.

"What the hell is wrong with you idiots? Do you think that we're all here for some lovely-dovey reunion? You can save those for after I get what I want," Winter said, starting to lose her patience.

"You're just scared because no one is paying attention to you, aren't you!" Estella yelled, mocking Winter's fragile ego. She was just like her mother, a greedy, vain hag.

"Quiet, one more word out of you, and Jacob will put a bullet right between your eyes,"

"You're a monster! Don't you dare harm her!" Snow yelled, her anger fueled by Faye's words.

"If that is what you wish, then so be it," Winter said, surprising everyone in the room.

"What?"

"I said I wouldn't harm her. I won't harm anyone if you do as I say and come with me."

"Don't listen to her, Snow, it's a lie. You can't trust her, not after what she did to your mother," Faye said. "There's no telling what she'll do to us once she has you."

Her words echoed in Snow's mind. There was no way she could trust anything Winter said to her. She had to fight back, but she didn't want to put her loved ones in danger.

"You'd best stay quiet," Winter said, having Jacob point his gun at Faye. "That warning I gave to the other goes for all of you."

"No! She's right! You tortured my mother and killed my father!"

"Killed your father? Have you not understood anything I have told you since you came here? I have always said that you were created. You don't have a father. You never did."

"What?"

"We created you by using artificial insemination on Aurora. We didn't want to complicate things by dealing with an outsider. Your only family is your mother and me."

"Your mother was nothing more than a useful pawn until the day she gave birth to you. Before, she was obedient and did whatever I told her, but then you came along. Do you know that your birth was the worst day of my life? That's because, on that day, she developed a conscience. She cared about you, a thing whose only purpose was to take her place. I can't fathom it.

"It's because she loved me!"

"Loved you? How could she love something like you? You aren't even a proper human. There was no love in your creation, only numbers. Before you were born, she understood that, but that changed. Little by little, just being near you made her weaker!"

"Love doesn't make you weak! It fills you with the strength to protect those you care about!" Snow yelled, refusing to believe that her birth mother's love for her was wrong.

"Spare me the love is power speech. I don't care," Winter said, seeing what would come if she didn't stop Snow.

"Your mother was pathetic for caring about you. After we caught her, we experimented on her for several more years before she managed to escape. Yes, that's right, your mother managed to escape from us using her annoying purple flames. Do you want to know what I find funny about all of this? She never came back for you."

"Your mother escaped from this facility and had over ten years to take you back, but she didn't. She learned her lesson. Love is for the weak; you were nothing more than a weakness that had to be discarded. I bet she wishes that she had learned that back then. If she had, she would still be by my side."

"Shut up! You don't know what you're talking about! My mother loves me!" Snow yelled, refusing to believe that her birth mother would abandon her. That frizzy black-haired girl said that her mother had sent her. She wasn't abandoned! Her mother was still trying to protect her.

"Of course she does, and the sky is red. Believe whatever you want. It won't make it true. The truth is what we see right here and now. We're here, and your mother is not. I can't find a simpler way to explain that to you."

"I will believe that my mother cares about me! Just because she never loved you doesn't mean you get to take your anger out on me!"

"Anger? Do you really think that this is anger? No, I was overjoyed the first moment I laid my eyes on you. Your birth may have been the worst day of my life, but your return was my best. When I discovered you were alive, I knew I couldn't miss such a valuable chance."

"The moment I laid my eyes on you, I saw so much potential in your small body that I found myself thinking of all the possibilities your existence could bring. Despite everything happening now, I have learned so much since your arrival."

"The discovery of other magic users, new energy-harvesting methods, effects of long-term magic exposure on a human's body, and so much more. And this is only the beginning. In time, my research will continue to grow, and there will be no stopping me. Snow, you are a gift."

"I don't want to be any sort of gift to you. It's over. The building is burning. You can't keep us here."

"Can't I? I'm more than certain that Jacob will be a good little pet. Staying here to make sure that you can't escape. But no, I'm certain that you will agree to come with me because of your foolish, caring heart. You can't bear to see anyone get hurt. You can't—huh?"

In the middle of her offer, Mochi began to attack Winter's leg, using his tiny bunny paws, though it didn't look like it was doing any damage.

"Get away from me, you stupid rabbit!" Winter yelled, kicking Mochi in his face. "Ugly thing had it com—agh!"

During the split second that she was distracted, kicking Mochi away, Autumn grabbed the gun out of her hands and punched her straight in the face.

"Don't underestimate me!" Autumn yelled, pointing the gun at Winter.

"Go, Mom!" Snow shouted, noticing the startled expression on Winter's face as she held her bleeding nose.

"Now you're going to put your gun down, and you're going to help me get these girls out of here," she said, smiling over to Snow. "Don't worry, girls, the nightmare is over. It's time we—ack!"

Just as quickly as Autumn had taken the gun from Winter, she was stabbed in the gut by a hidden blade in Winter's sleeve.

"You little—"

In a moment of horror, Snow felt as though her heart was going to stop as she watched Autumn crash to the ground, a streak of red following after her.

"Sorry, what were you saying?" Winter asked, wiping her nose before going to pick up the gun that

Autumn had dropped before shooting her straight in her left shoulder. "Something about getting out of here?"

"Mom!"

"Quiet!" Winter yelled, kicking Autumn in the face before making her way over to Mochi. "Did you really think that you and this thing had a chance to change things? I didn't do a background search on you for nothing. Your little escape attempt was all for naught. Though I really do hate pesky things that get in my way."

Winter placed her heel on top of Mochi's neck, and without a moment's hesitation, she crushed him.

The sound of Mochi's neck snapping filled the room. Snow looked over and saw Faye's expression of despair. He died trying to protect them.

"I'll kill you!" Faye yelled, nearly charging at Winter, but Snow held her back, relieved to see that Autumn was still moving.

"Enough, your time will come. And you, did you really think that grabbing my gun would save you? None of this had to end in bloodshed. You can only blame your own foolishness."

"Ngh! It's okay, girls. She only grazed my shoulder," Autumn said, trying to calm everyone down. "I'll be fine. There is nothing for you to—agh~!"

"Quiet," Winter said, pressing her heel into Autumn's bullet wound. "I am so sick of you idiots. Time and time again, you all find more ways to annoy me."

"Stop it! You're hurting her!" Snow yelled, tears rolling down her cheeks.

"And why would I do that? She asked for this. The moment she took my gun, she should have killed me, but she didn't. This is the weakness that all of you have. You are all too kind. None of you have the courage to do what needs to be done."

Autumn screamed out more as Winter twisted her heel inside of the wound.

"S-Snow, we have to stop her before it's too late," Faye said, her voice trembling from both fear and anger.

"It's actually sad how pathetic you all are, but you won't be seeing me shed a tear for you. In fact, I'm done playing nice. You know, at the beginning, I was planning on letting you all go if Snow was obedient and decided to stay, but it looks like she won't learn unless I show her the consequences of trying to defy me."

"Stop it! Get off of her!" Snow screamed, begging for Winter to leave Autumn alone.

"S-Snow, it's going to be alright. I promise," Autumn said to her, trying to comfort her daughter through the pain she was experiencing right now.

The air around Snow became colder and colder as the fear of what Winter was about to do began to overwhelm her mind.

"No, it's not going to be alright. I hope you're all glad because now little Snow gets to lose another mother," Winter said, pressing her gun right to Autumn's face. "I would say have fun in hell, but we all know there's nothing after death. Goodbye."

"Snow, you have to—"

"STOP! IT!"

Chapter 47

Icicles erupted from the ground, piercing Winter's gut and striking Jacob in the face, killing him instantly.

"Argh!" Winter screamed out in pain, dropping her gun to the ground while the others were too shocked to say anything.

"YOU! You want to know what real power is?" Snow asked, her voice sounding distorted and her eyes glowed. "I'll show you what real power is!"

"Agh!"

"Snow sweetie, stop!" Autumn yelled, realizing that something was wrong.

"Quiet!"

Snow's gaze was locked onto her. The moment their eyes met, Autumn felt as if the insides of her body were freezing over. She felt like she was going to freeze to death.

"Snow?" Estella couldn't believe what she was seeing. That ice came out of nowhere, but she was certain. She was certain that it came from Snow.

"Ack! G-good job, granddaughter," Winter said, coughing up blood, redirecting Snow's gaze back to her. "You win."

"Win? This isn't winning. I can't win until I make you suffer," Snow said, clenching her right hand into a fist.

"Agh!"

"How does it feel? That your body is freezing from the inside out. How does it feel to have your blood frozen bit by bit as it destroys you from the inside out? Go on, tell me. I need the data."

"Agh!"

Winter couldn't answer, only scream in pain. For years, she had subjected others to cruel and unusual torture without a care. Now, it was her turn to feel this pain.

"I'm sorry, we can't stop the experiment just yet," Snow said, freezing bits and pieces of Winter's heart. "It only gets worse for you if you don't talk. I wonder how it will feel if I start to freeze your brain?"

"Snow, stop! You're killing her!" Autumn yelled, terrified. She had never seen Snow like this before.

"Stop? Why should you stop?" Faye said, whispering in her ear. "She was going to kill all of us. She tortures us. She tortured your mother. She deserves to feel what we felt."

"Faye, stop it! Can't you see she's hurting?" Estella yelled, watching tears roll down Snow's face.

"I'm only telling her the truth. If you actually cared about Snow, you would let her do this."

"But—"

"ENOUGH!" Snow yelled, freezing everyone except Faye in place. "She must suffer! She must pay!

"Sn-Snow I—agh!"

Winter tried to speak, but Snow didn't want to hear a word of it. Before anyone realized what was happening, her eyeballs erupted from her skull, landing right in front of Autumn a second before she was ripped to shreds by the expanding ice.

The room was silent as Snow's ice returned to normal. Her revenge was over. Now she could go home. Now she could be… huh, why are they looking at her like that?

"Mom? Estella? Ember? She's gone. We're free," she said, taking a step closer to them, revealing a horrific sight. Behind her lay Terra, impaled by several dozen icicle spikes.

"NO~!" Ember shrieked, seeing her sister's mutilated corpse in front of her. "What have you done? What have you done!"

"N-no… I didn't mean… I only meant to help," Snow said, her voice trembling. "W-Winter is gone. We're safe now…"

"Safe? You murdered my sister, you monster!" Ember yelled, unable to cope with the stress of losing her sister only after just getting her back.

"N-no… that's not true! Mom, please tell her I wouldn't. Please! Mom!"

Autumn couldn't respond. Before Snow seemed like a sweet little Mochi that she would do anything to protect, but the thing before her now wasn't Snow. It was something else.

"Estella, please! Tell her!" Snow yelled, tears flooding from her eyes, but Estella wouldn't respond.

"You're a monster! A monster that destroys everything in her path! You deserve to die, not her!"

"N-no… I'm not… I'm not a monster!" Snow cried, begging them to believe her.

"Snow! Snow, look at me!" Faye yelled, forcing her to face her. "You did nothing wrong. You were trying to protect everyone, and you did. Terra was an accident, and I'm sure that she wouldn't blame you."

"Faye, you bitch! Don't you dare try to make it sound like it didn't happen! She's a monster! Kill her!" Ember yelled, overrun by her own grief to react appropriately.

"No, don't look at her. Look at me," Faye said, preventing Snow from glancing over at Ember. "These people can never understand what you just did for them, but they aren't like us. They don't understand the burden of carrying magic, but I do. And it's not just me. There are others, too. More people like us. These people see you as nothing more than a monster. If you come with me, you can be safe. If you come with us, there will be no more pain."

"Us?" Snow asked, feeling comforted by Faye's words.

She was right; she had tried her best to save everyone, and now they were looking at her as if she were some kind of monster.

"Yes, us."

A purple portal opened behind them as the frizzy black-haired girl from before emerged, covered in sweat.

"Yes, us. Despite her being late, she can take us away from here. She can take us to where we belong. She can take you to your mother. Your real mother. Not this woman who won't even offer a word of comfort or try to embrace you in your time of need. Just look at her eyes. She sees you as a monster, just like the rest. Her love for you was never true."

"You're right; no one loves me here. I need to go home, my real home," Snow said, walking toward the frizzy black-haired girl who gently wrapped her in her arms.

"It's okay, you're safe now," the girl said in a comforting tone.

"That's enough, Misty; help her through the portal. It's time for us to go home," Faye said, revealing that she had been working with her all along.

"No! Don't go!" Estella yelled, breaking the silence. Snow was hurting, and they treated her like a monster. She didn't want to drive her away. "Please don't leave. I love you!"

Snow slowly lifted her head as the portal started to close around them, looking at Estella one last time.

"Liar."

"SNOW!"

Acknowledgments

Writing this book has truly been an experience that I will never forget.

For those of you who don't know, this story started as a choose-your-own-path series on the site DeviantArt. My initial goal for the story was to give my community something special, something that they could be a part of.

As you read this, some parts may seem rushed while others might not make sense at first. However, everything was designed to give the character multiple choices, like introducing all of Ember's friends at the beginning. Every option was carefully considered to further the story in unique ways. This caused the story to branch far more than I ever expected.

To be honest, I never thought I was going to actually publish this story, but the more I wrote and the deeper I got into it, the more I knew I had to publish it.

I can't take all the credit for how this story turned out because it was my community that gave me each of these ideas; all I did was bring them to life. So, hopefully, if you're reading this, I thank you for the help you gave me in making this story.

And lastly, and certainly not least, I want to thank the reader for picking up and giving Snow Dust a chance. Your support means everything. I'm so excited to have had the chance to share this world with you.

Josh Decker

is a creative author of fantasy. He seeks to create new worlds with his stories and is always thinking about what to create next after his first book, **Demon's Awakening**. He lives in New York surrounded by friends and family who support his dream to share his stories with the world.